USA TODAY BESTSELLING AUTHOR
SARAH BRIANNE
LUCCA II
MADE MEN

Young Ink Press Publication
YoungInkPress.com

Copyright © 2023 by Sarah Brianne

Edited by CD Editing
and Diamond in the Rough Editing
Cover Art by Young Ink Press

All rights reserved.

Connect with Sarah,
facebook.com/AuthorSarahBrianne
instagram.com/authorsarahbrianne
youtube.com/sarahbrianne-author
SarahBrianne.com

PROLOGUE

THE RETURN OF THE BOOGIEMAN

L ucca dropped the white paper bag covered in grease stains, letting it slip through his fingers. The second it hit the cold concrete floor, you could hear the harsh clanking of chains as the dirty creature crawled from where it had been hiding in the darkened corner and into the glow of the light.

Taking the metal chair from the wall, Lucca unfolded it and placed it in front of the ravenous being before he sat down. There were two feet of cold floor separating them— the first foot was for safety, but the second was for his nose, because not even the strong scent wafting off the bag could mask the stench.

The thing before him had once been human, even though his name, Lucifer, said otherwise, and while he had lived up to his name with his once wicked ways, he was still human, nonetheless. Now Lucifer Luciano, the former mob boss of the Luciano family, was closer to being an animal than a man.

It was fitting, Lucca supposed; he always thought made

men were just animals hiding beneath their expensive Italian suits. He knew it because ...

He was one, too.

He was known as the Boogieman of Kansas City, and there was no one left to rival his cruel reputation as his enemy now sat in chains. He figured, in another universe, the roles could be reversed. It might have been Lucca shoving the burger and fries down his throat as if he were a dog eating his last meal while Lucifer stood above him. Thankfully, however, in this world, that wasn't the case.

There wasn't much that could turn Lucca's stomach, but slowly watching the outside of Lucifer match the inside had been something else entirely. The transformation seemed to even resonate with a part of Lucca's own sick brain because ...

What lived in Lucifer lay dormant in him.

The sickness that lurked just below the surface only stayed there because he had taught himself control, letting it only seep out during opportune times, if it could bring him closer to his ultimate goal. Lucifer's, however, didn't ever live beneath the surface; his sickness cocooned him, only getting thicker with age. But now the hard shell had been cracked with Lucifer's loss of power, as Lucca had forced him out, blooming the disgustingly helpless creature into its final form.

The sight of it all should turn his stomach knowing he, too, could have ended up just like Lucifer ... but then he would remember *why* Lucifer had come to be here in the first place, and suddenly, the rotten smell of flesh became satisfying enough for him to move his chair a foot closer.

At the movement, Lucifer cowered mid-bite, only returning to his ravenous ways when his captor didn't make another move.

Lucca didn't have to do anything else. Having him cower before him was enough to satiate the thoughts that ran through his head.

It was the scars carved into a young girl that had brought them both here, inside this concrete room. Unluckily enough for Lucifer, the carvings he had cut into that young girl's porcelain skin many years ago had become the scars that Lucca had fallen in love with at first sight. That scarred girl was also the reason he wouldn't be the one on the cold, hard floor, because she alone kept the monster within.

With a last bite, Lucifer licked his fingers, sucking off any grease left behind, along with any crumbs left under his nails. Lucca could see that, like a starved animal, once his hunger was satiated, a trace of the old Lucifer returned to his black orbs.

"What's the occasion?"

"The occasion?" Lucca asked, not knowing what Lucifer meant while carefully noting a hint of his prisoner's old voice had returned, as well.

"The suit." Lucifer dropped his eyes to Lucca's all-black, custom-made garment. "I've only seen you wear it a handful of times ... when the Boogieman has business to attend to."

A sly smile began to touch Lucca's lips.

"So, what's happened to grace us with the return of the Boogieman?" Lucifer asked again with hopefulness in his voice.

Ah ... Now I understand.

Lucifer was right; there was no hiding the monster underneath when he was dressed to kill. When he wore the black suit, the Boogieman came out to play.

Lucca reached into his pocket and pulled out a pack of

cigarettes. He gave the bottom a hard hit before he removed a stick and placed it between his sneering lips. "Today isn't the day you die, Lucifer."

The old Lucifer vanished, and in its place, the creature returned. *"When?"* it wailed as it began begging at Lucca's feet. "When are you going to finally fucking kill me?"

"Your body might belong to me," Lucca said, lighting the end of the cigarette, the glow from the flame dancing over his handsome face, "but your soul isn't mine to take."

Lucifer hadn't been a fearful man before he'd entered this cell, but that was all that remained of the man he'd once been. Now, fear dripped out of his every crevice, because if Lucca was saving him for someone else, then that was a person he didn't want the misfortune of meeting.

The prisoner gave up, and his chains rattled as he flung his back to the ground and lay there, helplessly wishing for death.

That was just no fun for Lucca.

Rising from his chair, he placed it back against the far wall, in its place.

Lucifer turned his head from where he mindlessly stared up at the concrete ceiling to the leaving back of his captor. "You didn't tell me the special occasion," he commented curiously, glaring at the suit. Even though Lucifer Luciano was a piece that had been wiped off the board in the mafia world, he was always going to want to know if he had been a part of the winning or losing side.

Inhaling deeply on his cigarette, Lucca spun on his heel. Then, as a smoky cloud escaped with each word, he said, "That's right. You haven't been able to hear the good news."

It wasn't the creature that waited on bated breath for Lucca's next words but the once Luciano mob boss.

"Kansas City has a new king ... and you're looking right at him."

THE DAY I AM MADE

LUCCA, AGE 17

L ucca stared at the closed sign on the Italian restaurant then checked his watch, having to move up the sleeve of his new, all-black Italian suit that he'd had made especially for today. It was a special day, and he'd decided to dress for the occasion.

He adjusted the heavy duffle bag back on his shoulder, wishing he had time for a cigarette. However, the insistent groaning beside him reminded him he didn't.

Taking a deep breath of air, Lucca remembered the promise he'd made himself this morning.

Today will be the day I am made.

Lucifer and his men filled the entire restaurant as he sat at the table next to his underboss, Anthony, and his oldest son, Dominic. His nineteen-year-old son was only a year into being a made man, and even though he was a quick learner who held a lot of promise, it wasn't the kind of son *I wanted*. Unlike him, he felt emotions, and in this business, you were better off without them, 'cause feeling anything but powerful ... *made you fucking weak.*

The *ding* from the bell above the door should have caught their attention, but it was the sound of something heavy being dragged in that had every Luciano turning their heads to find a body being heaved in. Every gun would have been drawn if it weren't for the one who was doing the dragging. You see, it wasn't the shock of who was being dragged in that held them all in place but because of *who was dragging him in.*

"Lucca Caruso," Lucifer drawled out his name with a sinister smile as he looked him up and down. "My, my, don't you clean up nice."

Usually, his adversary, Dante's firstborn son, ran around looking like he belonged on this side of the tracks, but they were all quickly reminded just how old he had gotten and which side he stood on based on his expensive suit alone.

"I solved our little rat problem," he said, dropping the body and duffle bag on the ground with a hard thud.

Our? Lucifer's eyes slightly narrowed. He was only seventeen; there was no way ... "Were you made, kid?"

"No." Lucca's strange eyes shifted from green to blue. "But I will be after this."

They were shocked to find the man beaten to a pulp was still alive when the kid grabbed a fistful of hair to bring his face off the ground and ripped the duct tape off his lips.

The man instantaneously started running his mouth. It was like hearing a pig squeal for its life.

"I'm sorry, Lucifer. but I got pinched, and they were telling me I was facing twenty years! I didn't want to snitch anymore, okay? So, I thought it would be mutually beneficial for all of us if I got my hands on enough cash to get the hell out of he—"

Blood spurted like a hot geyser out of the side of his neck when Lucca's blade entered his throat to the hilt. Slowly, he dragged the knife to the other side of his neck, slicing him from ear to ear as more blood flowed out, turning from a geyser into a river.

When the last breath of life had been taken, Lucca released his grip and the lifeless head fell to the ground, causing some of the blood to splash up on his young face.

"Odd how the rat was from your family, but the stolen cash was Caruso money."

Like everyone else, Lucifer could only stare in awe as Lucca picked the duffle bag up and threw it over his shoulder.

"Anyway, I guess I'll be seeing you around, then."

"Oh, you will," Lucifer said with a tilt to his lips, certain they had just witnessed history being made and, next time he saw the kid, he'd be made. *That, I'm sure of.*

He watched the kid leave into the night like he had entered as if he were the boogieman, and even though only two years younger than his own son, Lucca Caruso was going to be the youngest man to ever become made and ...

That was the son he had wanted.

FROM CHILD TO MAN

"He's still a child!" he heard his mother cry from the other room.

"We both know Lucca is far from a child, Melissa," Dante said calmly, under no disillusions of what exactly his son was.

"He's still only seventeen!" she wailed. "I thought you couldn't be made till you were of age?"

"The only rule is a *child* cannot be *made*, and what he did"—he paused for a brief moment, as if picturing the things his son had done—"no longer constitutes him as a child."

Even though Lucca couldn't see them from the other side of the door, he could still hear his mother's tears as they fell upon her cheeks. When the door flew open, however, nothing would prepare him for the look in his mom's eyes ...

"Mom, please." Lucca rolled his eyes heavenward. *It didn't matter how much he dragged his feet, he still found himself*

going farther and farther down the aisle as they passed each pew.

"That demon is coming out ..."

He couldn't help but laugh, knowing it was one of their inside jokes. She didn't mean any harm by it because, everyone but his mother believed him to be a lost cause ...

"I see the goodness in you, and no matter how much you pretend you don't, I know you have a heart, Lucca."

Sure, he did, but figuratively speaking, it didn't mean he felt the way everyone else did. And while he felt more for his mom than any other person, it was nothing compared to how she felt for him. He wished he could return even half her love, but he was thankful she didn't hold it against him that he couldn't. He did what he could to make her happy, though, by spending time with her while she taught him to do her favorite things—gardening and cooking—which seemed to be enough for her.

But, as they drew closer to the confessional, his voice echoed across the church. "This is stupid!"

Mellissa suddenly stopped as her emerald gaze bore into him. "Saving my son's soul could never be stupid."

THAT HAD BEEN the first time his mother had taken him to confession, and it was just a week ago when she'd dragged him to his last. Both of them now knew it, yet Mellissa still went to her knees, begging for him to go confess his sins, knowing where he was going and what he was about to do ...

Lucca took both of her hands in his, holding them as tensely as he held her emerald gaze. "Mom, there's no saving me after what I did." His words were not only clear in tone but in meaning.

It hadn't hurt to say it, but it shocked him that it did

hurt when his mother could finally see that he was right. For her to see that her child was no longer a child but *a demon* after all.

"Ready?" Dante spoke softly after watching Melissa wipe her tears as she walked away. It was clear the battle between being a good husband and proud father was beginning to take its toll.

Lucca nodded. It was time to take his code of silence and speak the omerta as he went from child to man.

LUCCA, AGE 18

THE SUN WAS SETTING as he walked through the garden, the colorful flowers swaying in the gentle breeze. He approached his mother, seeing she was on the ground, fussing with the herb part of the garden. Thankfully, Melissa was the kind of mother from Christmas movies and children's books, the kind of mom who could even love a monster. So, while she had now seen the true evil in him over this past year, she still loved him the same as when she had first laid eyes on him after she had birthed him.

Attending church was no longer something they did together, but he tried to make up for it by spending any extra time he could with her in the kitchen, cooking, or in the garden, gardening. After being made, though, it wasn't as much time as he liked, but it was still the only way he knew how to return her love.

"I thought you told me not to garden when you're too stressed or emotional; otherwise, they won't grow?" he teased his mom at seeing the bit of stress on her features.

"It's true." She laughed at her own words. "Nero is just

a bit sick, so I came out here to get him some mint for tea, but a rabbit must've eaten some for lunch."

"Ah." He nodded, understanding now. He got on the ground and began to take over. "I'll fix this up while you go fix him some tea."

"Thank you." She smiled at him, and the stress washed away from her almost immediately before it returned when she got a good look at him. "Lucca, when was the last time you got some sleep?"

He decided not saying anything was better than telling her he had yet to sleep in the last twenty-four hours, and there was no point in lying because she always knew when he did.

Melissa took a deep breath. "You're putting too much pressure on yourself to be something you don't have to be."

Usually, he was silent in the matter, always letting her say her piece, but his lack of sleep didn't want him hearing this conversation for the millionth time. "Mom, please."

"I'm just saying, you don't have to follow in your father's footsteps, is all," she reiterated.

"It's not his footsteps I'm following ..." he finally explained, his voice turning dark. "This is who I am." It didn't matter if his father was the mob boss of the Caruso family or not; Lucca would one day become the king of Kansas City, even if his father were a tailor.

"No, you're much more," his mother assured him sweetly, tucking a fallen strand of hair back behind his ear. "One day, you'll understand when you have your own children why I only want the best for you and why I refuse to believe you're no longer worth saving, like you think you are."

"If you knew the things I've done, you wouldn't say that," he mumbled under his breath.

"You think I don't know?" she revealed. "You forget who took you to all your therapist and psychiatric appointments."

"I remember. Just didn't think you wanted to believe them."

"I didn't have to be told there was something different about my children; that's why I took you in the first place. Mothers can sense when something is wrong with their child. Stomachaches or colds might be easier to recognize, but that doesn't mean we don't notice your interactions with others. I wanted to get you the help I could while you were still young enough to make a difference."

Lucca suddenly ceased what he was doing. He hadn't known that.

"And then I stopped taking you and Maria when I got scared they would label you both dangerous to others and break their code of confidentiality."

He wasn't sure at which age it was that he had been diagnosed with ASPD (Antisocial Personality Disorder), but he was sure it was quite alarming for her to find out two of her four children were fucked in the head. The verdict was still out on his younger brother, Nero, as he was only twelve, and while it was obvious there was something up with him and Maria at that age, Nero appeared to be different. He had flashes of darkness every now and then, but it was nothing compared to his.

Their youngest brother, however, was perfect. Even as a baby, it was obvious how much Leo was going to take after their mom. Lucca remembered being happy for the first time in his life when he had realized it, grateful that their mother would at least have one normal child, because she definitely didn't deserve the other children their father's genes had given her.

"You see, I'll always do my best to protect you in this life *and the next.*"

He didn't believe in such things, *but if there was* ... "I don't think we will be going to the same place."

"I've been taught that any man, no matter what they've done, can seek salvation, and you, my son, are no different."

"Mom, I've told you—"

"I understand that salvation isn't going to come to you by going to church ..."

Lucca stared into her eyes and saw she wholeheartedly believed every word she was about to say.

"You'll find your salvation in a woman, just like your father did." She smiled proudly at him, as if she could see the future.

Doubtful. While his father clearly had the heart for love, Lucca didn't. He never could see himself falling head over heels for a woman, like Dante had.

Practically hearing her young, naïve son's thoughts, Melissa laughed as she tucked a strand of his hair back behind his ear again. "Oh, I have every faith you'll find the love of your life one day, *but* you might want to get a haircut first so you don't scare her away."

Plucking some mint leaves, he handed them to his mother, not having the heart to tell her he'd never do such a thing, as it would make him weak, just like it had made his father weak. As the king of Kansas City, the less you loved, the better. That was the one thing—the *only* thing—Lucca had been born to do.

"For Nero's tea."

"Right." She nodded, dusting her hands off before taking them. "I need to run to the store to pick up some soup for him real quick. Would you mind staying here and watching your brothers until I get back?"

He began dusting his own hands off. "I can go pick up some soup—"

"No." She shook her head. "You finish that then go be with them. You haven't seen Leo, Nero, and Maria in a while, and they've missed you."

He didn't know why, but his hands wavered before digging back into the dirt.

Every made man was given a penthouse at his father's Casino Hotel, and so he had been sleeping there most nights. It had been a few weeks since he had been home, too busy assuming the responsibilities of being a soldier to return.

"Okay, then I'll stay," he finally agreed.

"Good." She happily smiled and got up. "Oh, look, the sun's setting," she noticed, her attention diverted once again by the beauty of the sky. "Come sit with me for a few minutes."

Lucca dusted his hands off once again before following his mother to her favorite spot in the garden. The white gazebo lights flickered on, as if on cue, as they sat underneath them together on the bench their father had order for her.

The two of them sat in the garden until the sun had set, the stars now beginning to twinkle in the sky above. His mother then left with the sun. It was a moment Lucca would soon treasure forever, not knowing it would be their last time together in this place or on this earth, as Melissa was soon set to depart.

Being gunned down in the grocery store parking lot wasn't how anyone had pictured Melissa Caruso going down, but it was as if Lucca had always known his mother's time here on earth was limited. She was too pure and good for this city, and having something that delicate married to the mafia could only mean one thing.

His mother was always Dante's one and only weakness, and all his enemies knew it. Lucca knew it because he planned to one day sit on the same throne his father did.

It was exactly what he would have done if he wanted to take it.

LITTLE PSYCHOPATH IN THE MAKING

LUCCA, AGE 18

O ne word flashed through Lucca's mind since his mother's death.

Kill.

And after burying her, the voice only got stronger.

It had turned out his father was fucking weaker than he'd thought. Lucca knew exactly who had killed his mother, and even though he hadn't pulled the trigger, that didn't mean he wasn't the one responsible for Melissa being six feet in the ground. Dante, however, needed "proof" to start a war between the two families, but what did proof matter? The Lucianos were the only thing that threatened the Carusos' hold on this city. After the last war, yes, there had been a lot of casualties, but in the end, the Carusos' victory had been hard fought, taking most of the city as theirs while they gave the Lucianos the shit part of it that none of them wanted to step their Italian leather shoes on, anyway. The next war could result in the Lucianos' extinction ... and that was exactly what Lucca planned for now.

His Escalade bumped high over the railroad tracks, and the bright lights of the city quickly dimmed the deeper he drove into Blue Park. You were lucky to find a light post working properly on this side of town; they were either completely out, flickering on their way out, or shined a yellowish-brown tint.

Cutting his light, he pulled over a few houses down from the one Sal had given him the address to. He took the time to put a cigarette to his lips and light the end with one of his matches he always picked up from the bar of the Kansas City Casino Hotel. Taking a few draws, he scoped out the house. Nothing—absolutely *nothing*—could have prepared him for the state of it.

It was the stark opposite of the house he had grown up in. His white mansion was surrounded by a garden; this one was a shack, to put it nicely, that barely held a blade of grass under the litter surrounding it. Normally, he wouldn't have given a single fuck about the state of a house, but this one resonated with him because it supposedly held the same amount of children his had. He couldn't imagine Nero or Leo living in a place like this and, God forbid, his sister, Maria. It was like seeing how his life could have turned out if the Caruso-Luciano war had had a different outcome ... and he actually might've given a tiny fuck *if* Lucifer hadn't killed his mother.

Speak of the devil.

Watching Lucifer exit the shabby house, he could practically see the steam coming out of his head. Whatever had just happened inside couldn't have been good, which made Lucca grateful for who his father was for the first time. While Dante wasn't the best of fathers, he wasn't the devil, at least, and it was obvious that even Lucifer's own children weren't safe from him.

The end of his cigarette glowed brighter as he watched Lucifer draw closer to the car. Lucca didn't know exactly what he planned to do tonight, as it ranged from torture to murder at the moment. A million different sights of the devil being in pain flashed through his mind as he gripped the steering wheel, trying to keep himself in place, and just as his grip loosened ... the Luciano boss headed back to the house.

Would he come back out?

Maybe he had just forgotten his keys?

Had he missed his one and only chance?

Lucca's eyes were pinned on Lucifer, seeing him now bang on the door of the old, beaten-up house. Every instinct he had told him something bad was about to happen to the family inside that home, and he was proven right once that door was finally flung open. He got to witness it all through that open doorway as he started to watch each of the Luciano brothers fall.

The younger twins fell quickly, but it was Dominic, the oldest, who put up a brave fight. He took note of the future Luciano mob boss and realized that, if it came to a fight between them, Lucca would have to fight dirty, like Lucifer. So, why did he find himself getting out of the car to go help him? Just moments ago, he had wanted everyone who carried the Luciano name to be put six feet under with his mother, and now he was about to help his future's biggest adversary ...

A small shadowy figure came out from behind the house and started walking down the street. Lucca's attention now drawn to it, he found himself following at a distance, his instincts telling him this was more important. When it veered off toward a children's park that had been overrun by the less fortunate, he let himself get closer, and his interest was suddenly piqued.

It was a child, a young boy, who had walked off into

the scary dark night. To any other kid, this place would have been frightening to such a young mind, but he supposed this was far less scary than the house he had just left.

He inched closer and closer once the kid had taken a seat on the dirty old swing set. At first, Lucca thought he looked sad that no one was there to push him, but the second he got close enough to see that his foot had stomped on a spider on the ground and he was now watching the half-alive creature being tortured, he realized what that expression on the kid's face was ...

Boredom.

"Hello." Lucca finally let his presence be known once he took a seat on the swing beside him.

"Hi."

The little shit couldn't be less afraid of him.

"What's your name?" Lucca asked, as if he didn't have a fucking clue, even though it was more than obvious who this little psychopath in the making was who looked like a pocket-sized version of Dominic.

The boy looked at him as if he should know who he was. "Cassius."

Lucca started to gently swing with a smile on his lips. He was indeed exactly who he'd thought. "It's nice to meet you, Cassius." He watched as the young boy went back to staring at the tortured spider.

Cassius was the last son born to Lucifer Luciano, and it looked like the devil had finally perfected his offspring.

"What are you doing out here so late?"

"My father is trying to hurt Kat again."

His ears perked up at hearing a name he hadn't yet known. Sal had broken down the Luciano family tree, along with any acquaintances the hacker could get his hands on, but he knew distinctly that he would have remembered a name like that.

"Who's Kat?" he asked, looking down to see what the boy was staring at.

"My sister."

Lucca almost couldn't believe it. "Oh." He was pretty fucking sure no one knew of Kat's existence, maybe not even Lucifer's men, and he was definitely fucking sure he was now the only Caruso to know.

There had to be a reason she was being hidden, but Lucca wasn't just going to find out more about the secret daughter; he was going to find out every fucking weakness the Lucianos had so he could wipe them off the crime family map when he became king. And the kid sitting next to him was going to be how. There was just one problem ...

Standing, Lucca crouched in front of Cassius, the moonlight illuminating the kid's face. On the outside, he might've been the spitting image of his older brother, but on the inside, they were as dark and fucked up as their father. And that was the problem.

"I like to hurt things, too."

Finally, Cassius looked back at Lucca. "You do?"

"Yes, but"—his shoe hovered over the tortured soul and then, as his shoe met the ground, he wished he didn't have to settle for just a measly spider for the night—"they must deserve it."

"Why?"

Lucca eerily felt like he was looking right into a mirror of himself at that age. "Because if we're not careful, we will end up hurting people like your sister."

Like my mother.

"I don't want to hurt Kat." Finally, some sort of emotion

showed on Cassius' face as the boy looked as if he had already done it.

"I won't let you. I can help you," he assured him, knowing he'd probably have to kill the bastard in the future.

"Okay ..."

The boy actually smiled up at him, and all he could think was, *What a dumb little shit. No one taught him not to talk to strangers?*

"What's your name?" the kid repeated.

Guess not.

"You can call me ..." Knowing he had him hook, line, and sinker, Lucca had to hide his smile, so he went behind Cassius and began to push his little body on the swing. Plus, it gave him enough time to think of an alias since this kid had the mouth of a dying wet rat. It wasn't like there were many Luccas around Kansas City, and as far as anyone was concerned, there was only one who mattered since his stint of becoming made. "Luke."

Cassius began to fly in the air. "Like *Skywalker?*"

"Sure, kid," Lucca huffed, hoping this better be fucking worth it. This plan was going to take years before it paid off. But boy, was it going to pay off when it did.

Lucca hadn't expected this night to turn out this way, and most of all, he couldn't believe he had almost tried to help the future boss of the Luciano family. He hoped Dominic was lying dead on that floor now, but something told him he wasn't going to get *that* lucky.

As he swung the little Luciano higher, a sneer lit his face.

He had already struck enough gold for one night.

HOW LONG HAVE YOU SMOKED?

LUCCA, AGE 20

S tanding in line at a gas station in Blue Park, he was down to his last couple of cigarettes. Lucca would have waited until he got back to his side of the city before he had gotten a new pack, but he planned on being on this side for a while today.

Lucca would turn twenty-one at midnight. Tomorrow was his birthday, and he was going to become the underboss, a position that was now being held by one of his father's best men and friend, Enzo, until he came of age. Everyone in the family had known this moment would come the second he was born, as only those who held the Caruso last name could hold the boss and underboss titles. Being his father's firstborn son, he was literally groomed to take over the family business, and now that he was turning twenty-one, he was about to be one step closer to becoming king. And, unlike his father, he planned on avenging his mother's death by destroying the Luciano family.

The only problem with becoming the underboss was that it came with more responsibilities, so his visits to Blue Park were going to become fewer and further between.

Over the years, he had grown accustomed to this side of town, sometimes even preferring it. Hell, he rarely wore a suit anymore because of it. His black T-shirt and jeans made him not only blend in around here but in Kansas City. No one recognized him as Dante's son, and it let him go places most Carusos couldn't without detection.

Somehow, Lucca had been lucky to not be caught by a Luciano in Blue Park, but it looked like his luck was about to run out ...

He had clocked Dominic the moment that little bell above the door dinged and he entered the gas station. Hell, he was impossible to miss. The oldest Luciano brother had filled out even more over the years, and even though Lucca was considered tall and fit, there was no comparison to the six-foot-five, muscled giant, which gave him even more reason to believe his time in Blue Park wasn't being wasted.

"Slumming it today, Lucca?"

Lucca turned, glancing down at the copious amounts of candy Dominic held in his hands, causing his brow to slightly rise. He had never had much of a sweet tooth, but maybe he should start adding Life Savers to his diet.

Hoping to keep this short and sweet, he shrugged before taking a step closer to the register as the line started to move. "Passing through."

Lucca didn't look back as the little bell jingled again, not wanting to face the Luciano more than necessary. However, he realized belatedly that he should have when a crazed man shoved past him and the older lady being waited on.

"Give me your fucking money!"

Goddammit.

Realizing the interaction with his adversary was no longer going to be short and sweet, he regretted taking the fucking drive over the train tracks once the gun was pointed at the cashier behind the counter.

Just hurry up already. His hand itched to reach for his gun, but the accomplice guarding the door kept him from blowing this guy's head off without casualties. Normally, he wouldn't care, but he still wanted to keep his visit to Blue Park somewhat of a secret.

As the robber tried to grab the cash out of the register as fast as he could, unfortunately, the cashier's oblivious son entered from a side room.

"Dad, I'm done. You—"

The now stunned robber turned his attention to the kid, ready to pull the trigger.

Somehow, Dominic closed the distance and pointed his own gun right in his face. "Put the gun down." Dom's cold voice cut even over the sound of a shot ringing out.

Unfortunately for Lucca, the accomplice had missed, striking the Luciano, who didn't even flinch, in the upper arm.

The next shot that rang out was from Dominic's gun as he splattered the robber's brains all over the store.

The accomplice finally realized who he had shot as Dom focused his sole attention on him. Then he realized just how fucking dumb he was when his eyes caught Lucca. Of all the gas stations to rob, it was clear he had picked the wrong one at the wrong time.

Now this is getting interesting.

Smiling to himself when the accomplice bolted, Lucca ran after him, not wanting Dominic to have *all* the fun.

When it was clear he wasn't going to be able to catch the Olympic runner, he finally pulled his gun from behind his back, wondering what kind of dumbass would rob a gas station wearing a bright-ass red shirt. The residents of Blue Park were about as bright as their lightbulbs.

"Don't. He's mine."

Before Lucca could sight that ugly red shirt, Dom had caught up to him and pulled the trigger of his own gun.

If he hadn't watched it himself, he wouldn't have believed that the Luciano could hit a moving target right in the head in a matter of a second.

Slowly, he turned in disbelief, pinning his eyes on his enemy. "You shot him in the head."

"Yes, I wanted him dead. I didn't think you'd be opposed to it."

Lucca did a double-take. That red shirt lay on the pavement what seemed like half a football field away. "But it only took you one bullet."

"Lucky shot." The future Luciano mob boss shrugged. "You could have saved me the bullet if you had caught him."

Pinning his eyes back, he knew Dom was trying to downplay his clear abilities with the Glock as he returned his behind his own back. "I don't know a man alive who could have caught that fucker."

"Maybe." Dominic smiled. "But you would've had a better shot of catching him if you'd put down the cigarettes once in a while."

Lucca could only let that comment slide, because it was probably true and because the cashier's kid, who had almost gotten his brains blown out, hurried up to them.

"I called my brothers. They'll help me clean up the mess up. You go. We'll take care of them."

What the—

Even more disbelief flooded him as he watched the red-shirted dead body being lifted into the trunk of a car.

Now that was something he hadn't seen before on this side of the tracks, or his.

When he heard the sirens, he quickly took out some cash from his wallet to buy the kid's silence about him being there, as it was clear he had already been trained well.

Lucca didn't even bother telling Dominic goodbye, knowing what he needed to do next as he jumped into his Cadillac.

Flicking over the engine, he pulled off, but he made sure to not speed up until the enemy was out of sight in his rearview.

It took him a bit to find the car that carried the dead body. He was actually about to give up when he finally spotted it pulling into a parking lot. The big sign that said *Money & King Funeral Home* told him exactly why it was being brought here.

Damn, Lucca had to fucking dispose of his *own* bodies. Countless nights he had spent burying bodies in graveyards. Meanwhile, he was pretty certain the residents of Blue Park would pick up the bodies for Dominic, probably to make some quick cash. Turned out they might not have been so dumb after all ...

Realizing he was late, Lucca drove off as night began to fall. Heading to the place where they had first met, he parked his car a bit down the road from the park in a rundown cul-de-sac. Certain his car wouldn't be seen if a Luciano drove by, he got out and started walking.

He heard shouting as he drew closer, and his instincts told him what was going on before he had even entered the sketchy playground.

He cut through the circle of kids to see Cassius sitting on a kid's chest as he repeatedly punched him in the face. He had seen that look on Cass's face before, but it had been years ago when they had first met—boredom. This time, it was much more disturbing to see because … how could the kid be bored in the moment? But it wasn't until a spurt of blood escaped the pinned-down kid's lip that something flashed across the youngest Luciano's face.

"That's enough," Lucca's sharp voice cut over the chanting. It was the fact that it wasn't much of a fight and more like a beating that had Lucca pulling Cass off him. "Show's over."

Cass fought being pulled off, but once he realized who was pulling him up, he finally got off the kid's chest and that crazed look in his eyes disappeared.

"He called me a little Luciano bitch, and then he went to steal my candy after he said he wasn't afraid of me *or my father*." He spoke a bit too evenly after just having been in an altercation.

It wasn't until the boy who had been mauled managed to stand up that Lucca noticed how much bigger he was than ten-year-old Cassius. This kid was around thirteen years old, so he had to have a few years on Cass, at least.

"Well"—Lucca looked at the older kid, who was now holding his bloody, broken nose—"how do you feel now?"

"I-I'm sorry," he cried through his tears. It was clear the kid had had a change of heart as he ran away in fear.

When he watched the boy trip over his shoes and fall flat on his face, both Lucca and Cass laughed.

"Who taught you to fight like that?" Lucca asked with a smile still on his face.

Cassius picked up the plastic bag that was full of candy as they headed for their spot on the swings. "Dom."

"Oh." Lucca stared at the candy that Cassius started to take out of the bag once they sat down. Most of them were the exact same ones Dominic had held in the gas station before the robbery had taken place.

"He got us this candy to share, too."

"Really?" Lucca should have known all that must've been for his siblings. He wiped the smile off his face. "Does he know about me?"

"I talk about you all the time to my brothers and sister, but I'm pretty sure they still think you're imaginary," Cassius revealed, opening a bag of gummy worms. "Want one?"

"No, thanks." He shook his head, craving only one thing. Pulling out the pack of cigarettes, he put his second-to-last stick to his lips before he lit the end with a match.

"How long have you smoked?"

It was the first time Cassius had ever asked about his smoking habits.

"A long time."

The kid seemed more disinterested in his gummy worms by the second. "Can I have on—"

"No." Lucca's firm voice stopped him from asking. Then he wondered what had garnered such a strong reaction out of him, knowing he hadn't been much older than Cass when he had put his first cigarette to his lips. He should be giving the kid a hit and hoped he died of lung cancer at a young age, but he decided that it was only the fact he only had one cigarette left as to why he didn't.

"Sorry, jeez." Cassius's interest returned to his gummies.

"Has your brother taught you anything else?" Lucca asked, changing the subject back to the reason why he ever crossed those train tracks.

"Yeah, he's going to teach me to shoot soon. I can't wait." Cass popped a worm into his mouth. "It's not fair I've had to wait so long, 'cause Dad taught him how to start shooting when he was five."

"Five, huh?" Lucca's brow rose. "So, he must be pretty good, then."

"Pssht, he's better than good. He can shoot through the middle of an O in a Coke can from like here to"—he looked around until he pointed at a dirty, old shoe far, far in the distance—"there."

Lucca laughed. "That's impossib—"

"No, it ain't. I've seen it with my own eyes," Cass told him dead serious, and Lucca knew he was telling the truth.

His brows furrowed as he checked his watch.

"You need to go?" Cass asked with a hint of disappointment.

"No, I can stay a bit longer." Lucca got back to their conversation, no matter how badly he wanted to leave to go see something. "So, why did your dad teach Dom to shoot so young but not you?"

"Well, he always said he wanted an army, so he taught us different things. Dom got to learn how to shoot, and then Angel, he taught how to use a knife, which made Matthias beg to learn the same thing Angel was doing."

"And you?" Lucca asked.

"Dad wanted me to learn everything off the bat," Cass said proudly at first. "But Dom somehow talked him out of it."

I can't imagine why.

"That's a shame," Lucca lied through his teeth, sure Dominic knew the same thing he did—that this city didn't need two Lucifers running around armed.

"Dom said I needed to focus on one skill at a time, so we're working on fighting first."

"Clearly," Lucca complimented, staring at Cass's still bloody knuckles.

Cassius ripped a head off a gummy worm with his teeth. "Soon, he'll teach me how to shoot, though, I'm sure of it."

God, let's hope not, Lucca thought, looking at his watch again.

"It's okay if you need to go. Dom told me not to be out too late after dark, anyway."

"You sure?" Lucca pretended to ask if it was okay, knowing he was going to talk his way out of leaving soon, anyway, if he was going to do what he needed to in time.

"Yep." Cass threw the leftover gummies back into the plastic bag before he jumped off the swing. "See you same time next week?"

"Actually, I needed to talk to you about ..." Lucca's words trailed off once Cassius's face fell. Suddenly, he didn't have the heart to tell him that he was going to be too busy with a new job and his visits to Blue Park were no longer going to be weekly. "Sure, kid."

Putting out his fist, Cass smiled.

Lucca bumped it before they did their secret handshake that a once littler Luciano had come up with on their third meeting.

As he started to walk home, Cass yelled, "Bye, Luke!" over his shoulder before he disappeared.

Shit. Lucca stood still then started walking, counting his paces. He almost lost count due to his distracted mind. Truthfully, he was no longer so sure if he was capable of killing the kid. With each visit, he got to learn something new about his enemies that he could one day use to take them down, but it also meant he grew closer to the Luciano each time. Cassius happened to be the same age as Leo, and while he was nothing like his sweet little brother, he was starting to see him as one.

Once the count got too damn high, Lucca stopped, his mind already too heavy. He closed the distance without the counting, his blue-green eyes piercing down at the dirty Nike-checked shoe.

One thing was for certain; *Cassius may not die ...*

Lucca kicked the shoe, sending it flying through the dirt. *But Dominic will.*

And when Lucca went back to the funeral home, getting lucky that the body hadn't yet been incinerated, he found that the bullet Dominic had fired had gone through the back of the head and right between the eyes of the accomplice. That was when he decided, *Dominic Luciano will definitely die.*

Hell, he was probably now his biggest and only threat for the throne, so his name shot up to the first on his list for avenging his mother, and now ...

Lucca just needed the crown.

THE GLOCK AND GOD HAD SPOKEN

LUCCA, AGE 26

"Hey, darlin'." The moment Lucca's eyes landed on Chloe's scarred face, all his plans came crumbling down. The need for revenge was gone, and in its place was only one need ...

To protect.

It was almost poetic that the man who had given her those scars was none other than Lucifer Luciano, and it was even more so ironic now that the Luciano mob boss, who was no more, lay rotting away where only Lucca could find him.

With her monster gone, he was finally able to say the words, "Marry me, darlin'."

Lucca knew then what he had to do. He had to do everything his father hadn't so he could protect his future wife, because burying Chloe in the ground, like he had his mother, wasn't an option. And God forbid, if she lay in a casket for anything other than old age, the world would certainly pay.

Lucca had finally realized what all his other predecessors hadn't—the weight of the crown must be shared. He just thought he would have some time for his plan to be set into motion, but little did he know someone else had plans of their own ...

Whistling, he strode up to the body that lay flat on the ground, careful not to step in the puddle of blood that was beginning to pool before he used his Italian leather shoe to flip the hefty body over.

It was a clean shot, straight through the back of the head, exiting right between the eyes. He had expected no less, even though a Glock wasn't his favorite gun of choice. But he needed them to think it was Dominic Luciano who had taken the shot. Now all he had to do was dump the body in the alleyway behind the Casino Hotel for them to find.

He stared down at the desolate eyes. The schmuck had had no idea it was coming, and that was how he liked it. When a hit was made, he took only one chance to make it, making sure there would be little error. And, if for some reason the shot was missed, then he took it as a sign of God's will that it wasn't that person's time to depart this earth.

Poor Tom. The Glock and God had spoken.

Tom would be the first casualty of many to come, but it wasn't the first Caruso life he had taken, and just like the last, he planned for a Luciano to take the fall.

Now let the war begin ...

THE DEATH OF A FRIENDSHIP

L ucca sat on the swing set, waiting.

He looked at his watch. These days, Lucca could only meet once a month, and it was thirty minutes past. He would give it a few more minutes, even though he knew Cassius wasn't going to show even before he had driven down to Blue Park.

It would be their first time meeting since `...

THE SECOND LUCCA CROSSED THE LUCIANOS' home's threshold, his cold blue-green eyes landed on Cassius.

He could see the shock in his now teenage eyes before realization dawned in them, now knowing his friend, Luke, had actually been Lucca Caruso this whole time. It was as if you could see everything Cass had ever told him that could be used against his family swim in his eyes.

The reason why Lucca was here in the first place was the last to shine through their depths, and it was as if Lucca could read the young mind.

Kat.

Anger was the last thing that flashed across Cassius's face before Lucca turned to look at the Luciano women lining up. It took him all of five seconds to glance down the line and know she wasn't among them. Every unmarried Luciano woman over the age of eighteen was supposed to be lined up, but there was one missing, and it was the only one who mattered. The only one who would set his plan into motion.

He might have never seen Lucifer's daughter, but his son had sure told him enough about her. Enough for him to pass right by the line of women and the new head of the Luciano family, Dominic, to go snooping around the shabby house. Supposedly, she had baby pink hair that she dyed, and if that wasn't a dead enough giveaway, the dead black eyes were when he found her hiding in the basement.

Offering her to Drago to marry meant any friendship and trust he had built with Cassius over the years would die in an instant, and yet ...

Lucca did it, anyway.

THE CHAINS of the rusty old swing set rattled when he stood. He headed for the park exit, but his steps ceased at the silhouette that appeared in the distance.

His gaze met the eyes of the young boy he had betrayed. He knew Cass had looked up to him as if he was another brother, and yet Lucca had stabbed him in the back without a moment's hesitation.

Over the years, he'd trained the youngest Luciano to follow his monstrous footsteps instead of his father's, and like Lucca, who had a soft spot for his mother at that age, he had a soft spot for his sister. So, to say he had betrayed him in the worst way possible was an understatement.

Lucca went to open his mouth, but before he could form the words, Cass shook his head.

"*Don't,*" he mouthed. Then, before he knew it, Lucca was watching the silhouette's back as he walked away.

Cassius had come there for one reason and one reason only—to tell Lucca what he himself already suspected.

The death of a friendship.

CLOSING HIS EYES, he rubbed his temples, missing that his office door had quietly opened.

A soft hand brushed his hair back. "What's wrong?"

"Nothing." His eyes finally opened to see his black-haired beauty had snuck in on him. As he grabbed her, Chloe trustfully allowed herself to be drawn down onto his lap so he could hold her. He remembered how hard it had been to get to the point where he could touch her, reminding him of just how far they had come for her to be the one to initiate touch. "Just tired."

Once she was comfortable, she lifted a fingertip to trace under his eyes. "You sure?"

Lucca was finding it harder to keep Chloe in the light and away from his darkness. He always made sure to tell her just enough to know he wasn't a good person, but he left the details out of just how twisted he was. She knew he had been made at seventeen because of something he had done, but he had yet to tell her what exactly that was.

"You can tell me anything, you know that, right?" she said, almost reading his mind. It was her way of politely letting him know she knew exactly who she was engaged to, but Lucca knew she wasn't quite so sure she did. To actually hear the things he had done would change the way

Chloe looked at him, whether she thought so or not, because not in her wildest dreams could she think them up. Never mind if she were to witness them.

"I know," he told her. Picking up a strand of her silky hair, he began twirling it around his finger. "Someone put their trust in me a long time ago, and I broke it."

"Oh." Chloe seemed a bit surprised at first that he'd actually told her. "Did you mean to break it?"

Staring into her gray eyes, he decided to tell her honestly, "Yes." But he kept the part that he meant to break it the moment he'd met him to himself.

"Why?" she asked so simply.

Lucca had expected her to look at him differently, but she had yet to. So, he continued, "I did it to protect our future."

"I see." Chloe thought for several long moments with sadness crossing her features.

When it was apparent she felt bad that he had betrayed someone for her, Lucca leaned down to kiss the part of her scar that ran above her brow. "Don't worry about it, d—"

"I think," she interrupted him, "if you were friends and explain why you did it ... I'm sure they'll forgive you."

He lightly shook his head with a slight tilt to his lips. It was cute how much she wanted to fix it, but the truth was she had no clue how broken it was. "I don't think so, darlin'."

"I think you might be surprised." She smiled sweetly, with hopefulness in her depths. "It's hard to let go of a long-time friendship. After a while, you start to forgive and forget the thing they did that hurt you, and you remember all the other times when they were there for you. Just give it some time. I'm sure they'll come around."

"Thank you," Lucca said, taking her hand in his, knowing he was undeserving of her words.

As he stared at their intertwined hands, the fragileness within his grip brought a wave of disgust over him that he was even touching her. If Chloe knew the details of the things he had done, she would run screaming in terror. He was as brutal as she was gentle. Her love blinded her to the true extent of his cruelty and the power he wielded.

Raising her hand to his lips, he met her eyes and allowed the mask he lived behind to drop, exposing the true extent of his feelings for Chloe's eyes only. Lucca would never let himself have the luxury with anyone else in the room. It was certain that the fragile woman clasped in his arms was the Boogieman's one and only silver bullet.

Lucca glanced down at the modest top she was wearing and felt himself getting hard. Women regularly flaunted themselves, trying to catch his attention.

When he shifted her on his lap, Chloe turned to straddle him so she could run her fingers through his hair. Her simple black blouse was buttoned to her neck. One by one, he slowly undid the buttons until he could see the lacy bra underneath.

"Why are you staring at me like that?"

Lucca stared down at her captivating, scarred face. "Because you should be running from me instead of cuddling into me."

Her eyes twinkled up at him mischievously. "Would you run after me?"

Lucca pulled her closer to him, his eyes turning dark. "I would never stop. I would chase you to the ends of the earth."

The fact that Chloe didn't seem terrified showed him how good of a job he had done at masking his true nature.

Slowly, her hand trailed from his hair to his chest to unknot his tie. Loosening it, she slipped it off his neck to lay it on his desk. Her gentle fingertips then went to his shirt to release the top three buttons. "There. Do you feel more comfortable?"

Lucca's lips twisted wryly. "No."

"Why not?" Chloe seemed confused. "You should be able to breathe now."

He bent down to hover his lips over hers. "I haven't been able to breathe from the moment I saw you."

Flushing under his scrutiny, she met his mouth with hers, unable to deny him the kiss he so desperately wanted as he took her lips.

No matter how many times he kissed Chloe, the fire between them always flamed higher.

Lucca cupped her breast, kneading the flesh beneath the lacy bra. Brushing his thumb over the nipple he could see protruding out, he felt Chloe shudder beneath his touch.

"Are you cold?" He protectively started rubbing her back, trying to warm her.

"No."

Good. Going back to tantalizing her nipple, he dragged his tongue over her bottom lip before gliding it across the curve of her jaw to her ear. Lucca let her feel the warmth of his breath until he felt her shudder again before teasing her earlobe.

He was determined to use their lovemaking to tie her further to him. Each time he made love to her, he tried to steal another piece of her heart ... until there would be no Chloe without Lucca.

His hands went to her thighs, repositioning her so that she was fully straddling him. As he moved her, her skirt shifted higher, enabling him to see the silky peach panties she was wearing. Having yet to see her in anything but black, he was about as shocked to see her wearing any color as he was at the fact he liked it so much.

"Peach is my favorite fruit."

Chloe's face flamed at the insinuation.

Easing a lone finger under the silky fabric, he parted her to run it through the wetness waiting for him. Slowly, he withdrew his finger and sucked it into his mouth. "Ripe enough to pluck."

He lifted her to the desk then rolled her panties down so he was given a salacious vision of Chloe perched within his reach.

Caressing up her thighs, he moved his chair closer, bringing his mouth to her sex. Then, lowering his head, he nuzzled the clean-shaven mound over her sheath before dipping lower to savor her pure essence.

Clutching his shoulders, she gave a low moan when his tongue feathered over her clit, teasing her with the pleasure he wanted her to beg for.

He switched from teasing her sensitive pink flesh to letting his tongue take possession of the part of her body that would never know another man's touch. He heard Chloe's sweet moans of need as he stood and straightened to unzip his trousers.

"Come to me."

Obeying, she lifted her hips off the desk and onto his cock. Lucca had to grit his teeth as she settled on him. Her heat surrounded him as her hips pressed down, driving him higher. Lucca had to hold her still when he embedded his cock inside of her to the hilt.

Cupping her bottom, he raised her slightly then lowered her, repeating the same maneuvers of lifting her higher before allowing her to slide down. Chloe tried to resist his controlling movements, impatiently trying to build a faster momentum, which would have her climaxing too soon.

"Be patient," he coaxed. Firming his grasp on her hips, he regained control. A low laugh escaped him when he saw her frustrated expression.

He hooked a finger under the cup of her bra to bare a breast so he could see the nipple, which was just pouting to be sucked.

Sucking the pert flesh into his mouth, he lightly grazed the nub with his teeth, making Chloe jump on his cock as if she had been electrocuted.

"Easy, darlin'."

"That's easy for you to say," she complained with a whimper.

"Making love to you is never easy," Lucca said, releasing her nipple to nuzzle her breast. "It's like entering uncharted territory, never knowing if you're going to come out alive, or if there will be anything left to bury when it's over."

Her expression was filled with doubt. "Do you really feel like that?"

"Every time."

"I feel like that, too." Her forehead sank to his chest. "All the time."

Lucca buried a hand in her hair. "You're only supposed to feel like that when we're making love."

"I see how the women in the casino look at you, Lucca. I'm not blind," she confessed her insecurities. "Sometimes, I look over my shoulder to see if you stare back."

Lucca braced his hands on the desk behind him so Chloe would move backward. Using his thighs, he started rocking back and forth as she straddled him. He knew he had found her sweet spot when her soft screams filled the air. He waited until she stopped trembling before he tilted her head back so she would be forced to look into his eyes that now glowed mostly green.

Lucca started moving again. "The only woman I see is you. The woman who belongs to me. Will always belong to me."

With her eyes on him, Lucca released the control he had over his body. Climaxing, he linked Chloe's fragile hands with his, and when it ended, he didn't lift her off him, keeping his cock nestled deep within her warm heat.

"*Ti amo, tesoro.*"

"What does that mean?" she asked breathlessly.

The only four Italian words that mattered. "I love you, darlin'."

TWO DEALS IN ONE CHAPTER

"What is your game here, Lucca?"

Lucca stared at the man on the other side of his desk.

Dominic Luciano had come all the way to his home office to speak with him. Truthfully, he hadn't given him much of a choice. Lucca had taken everything away from the Luciano mob boss that hadn't already been taken.

The city was destined for Lucca.

Half of their money went to the Carusos, thanks to his father.

Angel now worked for Lucca, again thanks to Lucifer.

Kat was to wed Drago.

And still, it wasn't enough for Lucca, so ...

"What is it you want?" Dominic's hazel eyes glowered at him.

"You're right. I do know everything about you, Dominic," Lucca admitted. Just a few moments ago, Dom had told him that he probably did because he had secretly befriended Cassius. And now Lucca was going to tell him exactly how much he did know ...

"I know the things you went through in that house, how you were raised, and what you're capable of." Rising, Lucca walked to face Dominic so the man would understand the severity of his next statement. "You and I will burn this fucking city to the ground if we don't see eye to eye."

"So"—a strange look crossed the Luciano's face—"what are you saying?"

Playing chess for the crown, he'd had to reset his board the moment he'd met Chloe. A change of plans had been in order, and now it was time to reveal his grand plan.

"We work together, and when I get my father to step down, we run this city together ... fifty-fifty."

Laughter filled the air for several seconds until it died.

"You're fucking serious, aren't you?"

Lucca simply nodded, letting him know this was no joke.

"Why?"

The why didn't matter. The deal he was offering was all that did. There was no way he was telling him how important Chloe was to him if Dominic hadn't figured it out already.

"I have my reasons. Now, do we have a deal ... or not?" Lucca asked, stretching out his hand.

It seemed like an eternity passed while Dom contemplated before he finally spoke, "Call off my sister's wedding, and we will."

That's disappointing.

Lucca turned away from him. "No."

"You said fifty-fifty, and you've taken everything from me. Kat is the only thing I'm asking to get back. My profits and Angel, you get to keep. You don't even need her, anyway." Dom's voice turned desperate.

That was where he and the Luciano mob boss differed

—the Luciano mob boss *might* win in a fist fight against him, but Lucca would *always* win in chess. Dom only ever thought one move ahead, while Lucca contemplated his next ten.

"But I do." He placed a cigarette between his lips. "Making Katarina a Caruso ensures our deal and that you will never betray me."

It was as if you could see Dominic's face drop. *Checkmate.*

"What about me, though? I've taken loss after loss. What ensures *my* deal with *you*? You have to give me something that proves your deal is in good faith and that you won't stab me in the back one day."

"Unfortunately, the terms you agreed to are off the table until I replace my father, but besides those, what do you want?" he asked, flipping open his Zippo to light the end. The thing was ... Lucca already knew exactly what Dominic secretly wanted, even if Dominic himself didn't know yet. "Think carefully, Dominic. You only get one choice," he warned, making sure he'd ask for the right thing.

With a deep breath, Dominic made his choice, "Maria."

Lucca had to take a long, hard hit to keep himself from smiling. Poor Dominic didn't even know that was exactly what he'd hoped the Luciano would ask for. Of course, how could he know Lucca would sell his sister's soul if it came to it to protect Chloe?

"Deal."

It was obvious the Luciano couldn't believe Lucca had agree to it just like that, but he wasn't dumb enough to look a fucking gift horse in the mouth.

"Deal."

Shaking hands, they sealed the deal before either could back out.

From the outside, it looked like Dom had gotten the deal of a lifetime while Lucca had gotten the shit end of the stick. But, what Lucca had gained was simply priceless. He not only got an army to protect the person he loved, but he got *Lucifer's Army*. No one, not even One-Shot, was going to stand against that.

Lucca finally let himself smile, staring into the hazel depths of the only person who could ever rival him, who could no longer lift a hand against him the moment he married his sister. And Lucca was going to do everything in his fucking power to make sure it did.

I guess I don't have to kill you after all.

To say Maria finally choosing Dominic to marry was easy ... would be the fucking understatement of a century. All his planning had almost gone to shit the moment Maria had met Kayne, but Lucca held true to his word, doing everything in his power to make sure it did.

Unfortunately for Kayne, it came at the highest cost ...

"I'd like to reward you," Lucca said, standing next to her.

This was not only Maria's favorite spot in the city but the world.

Looking down at the glittering city from his office at the Casino Hotel, her emerald gaze could stare down below for hours. However, her attention could no longer be held by the city lights.

Whispering, she appeared to be in disbelief while still knowing exactly what was coming. "You're going to let me be made ...?"

Even better.

"How does consigliere sound to you?"

"You want to make me your equal?" Maria's disbelief only grew, but like a consigliere should be, she was smart enough to figure out quickly why he would do this.

A knowing smile lifted her lips. "You're smart, brother, but even I didn't expect that."

Lucca's brow rose. "Do you blame me?"

The fact was, Katarina marrying Drago hadn't changed much between the two families. They had wed, yes, but without any children to account for yet, divorce still existed as a possibility. Dominic loving Maria wouldn't even die with her death, so if Lucca was to make her his equal, it would secure the Lucianos' mob boss's undying loyalty.

"No, I can understand." Her gaze went back to look at the beautiful view, knowing Lucca would do anything to ensure Chloe's safety.

Well ... "What do you say, Maria?" Lucca slowly stretched his hand out. "Do we have a deal?"

Done looking at the city, she faced her brother head-on. "I want two things before I do."

Lucca dropped his hand, waiting to hear her conditions, knowing whatever she was going to ask for was certainly going to be interesting.

"No guards, but I will take a *driver* of my choosing to watch my back."

This first request was *not surprising* but also *surprising*. Maria had been guarded by Caruso soldiers and had been duping them her entire life. It was her version of a compromise that Lucca had no problem agreeing to, other than he felt sorry for the poor sucker who would be doing her bidding. It was going to take one hell of a man to not only protect his sister but to stand by her. The good news was he wasn't going to have to bribe one of his men to do it.

Lucca feared he wasn't going to get so lucky with the second request.

"And I want you to buy me a car," she said, smiling brightly.

His brow rose again, this time amused. "What kind?" But Lucca should have known it was a dumb fucking question ...

"Whatever one I want."

He knew it was going to cost him a small fortune with his sister's taste, but there was no price he wouldn't pay for Chloe's safety. "Deal."

"Deal." Maria shook his hand.

Making two deals in one chapter of his life made one thing for certain—the throne was running out of room to sit.

"Oh, and Lucca"—Maria, who was heading out the door, had stopped—"I know you've been secretly helping Cassius."

He couldn't help but smile. Maria would know what he had been doing better than anyone. Neither of them had anyone like them around when they were younger and, like Lucca, Maria had grown fond over the youngest Luciano since spending time in Blue Park herself.

"Unfortunately, in the process, you taught him to smoke." Her voice took on a rather threatening tone. "Now fucking undo it."

Well—All Lucca could hear now were Maria's expensive heels clicking goodbye—*shit*.

WHY THEY CALLED HIM ONE-SHOT

*O*ne-Shot, he whispered the name that had been bestowed upon him. He liked it, thought it was fitting.

I'm gonna get you ... so pray to our Father ... for if I miss ... I will only take one shot.

He had held true to that promise, taking many lives so far. Lately, though, God had had other plans, while his Glock ... well, some people just called for different measures to be made, and Maria Caruso had been one of them.

The bomb he had set had been meant for her, while it had taken the soul of another. Her bodyguard, Jerry, hadn't been the only casualty.

It hadn't been in his plan for Leo Caruso to be touched. He took no pleasuring in taking a child's eye. Children were not to be touched, because ... he was a Caruso after all.

And if there was anything he stood for, it was to ensure the rules and to keep the *old ways*.

Hell, it was why they called him One-Shot.

THE DAY HE HAD BEEN
WAITING FOR

LUCCA, 27

'L ucca, I'd like to talk to you alone for a moment."

When Lucca first walked into his father's office for the family meeting that his father had called, he had to admit he hadn't expected it to go that way. He had noticed his father was beginning to soften, but even he hadn't expected Dante could fall in love again. One thing Lucca never doubted was how much he had cared for Melissa, so much so he had never been the same after her death. He had forgotten what he had been like, just how much more palatable his father had been until he'd met Nadia. Thankfully, Lucca liked her, but it was going to make it harder for him to force his father to give up the crown.

Dante Caruso's time as the head of the family had come and gone, and everyone fucking knew it but Dante himself. Their family grew more at risk every day he sat on the throne, and it had already cost many good Caruso men's lives. Worst of all, it had cost Leo's eye.

One-Shot had taken too much from them, which had put a big bullseye on them, letting any enemy within a hundred-mile radius know the Caruso family wasn't what it had once been.

Lucca shut the door behind a pregnant Maria. He could barely hide his smile when she had told them she and Dominic were expecting. The bargain he had made with Dominic Luciano had already paid off, as now their futures intertwined and no longer because of war but due to love. Soon, their blood would mix, and once Lucca took the throne, the two families of Kansas City would be unstoppable.

He took a seat in a leather chair across from where his father sat behind his desk. Lucca desperately needed a cigarette after having to listen to what Dante had just revealed …

"YOUR MOTHER *and I had an arranged marriage. Her father owned this Casino Hotel and had received many offers to sell, but the only way he would agree to sell to my father was if his daughter married his son. That way, when he passed, this property would pass to me, which would be returned to his daughter, and then his future grandchildren."*

Lucca stood in the corner, flipping his Zippo open and shut as he listened to the story he had heard many times before when he was a child.

"However, even though her father and mother were, in fact, Italian … your mother was not."

He closed his Zippo with a loud click. The hair on his arms stood on end after hearing a part of the story he had never known.

"Who knows this?"

"Very few people ever did. Most of the ones who did are dead now."

Dante continued, now speaking to Maria and Nero as Lucca already knew what it meant. "If this information fell into the wrong hands, any future children you might have with Dominic, Elle, or Chloe—"

Lucca's eyes glowered as his met his father's ice-blue ones.

"—may never sit where I sit one day."

LUCCA HAD BEEN PREPARED for his future children to only be fifty percent Italian, but he hadn't been prepared for himself to be.

His father's words still swirled in his head. *"There will always be those who will never forget the old ways."*

Unfortunately, Dante was right. That, Lucca had known and prepared for. There was no changing the mafia rules they all lived and died by for many generations overnight. It was going to be a long, hard road ahead for the family, but Lucca also had a backup plan that was thankfully foolproof. His plan was *time*. That by the time his children had come of age, the old fucks who held on to those old ways *would be dead*.

Lucca had never understood Dante's indifference toward Chloe until that moment. Everything was beginning to make sense as to why his father was so against his children not marrying Italian blood, and it was because he wanted to protect the Caruso legacy.

Dante himself had already risked the legacy by having children with Melissa, and now all the Caruso children were playing with—

Lucca stared at the flame coming from the Zippo. *Fire.*

He took a long hit. He should kill his father for not

telling him this sooner. He could reach over the desk right now and strangle the fucking life out of—

The sound of the heavy crystal ashtray sliding across the desk had his thoughts of murder dissipating into thin air. His eyes narrowed on it. Countless times, he had entered his father's office, and not once had he offered up his precious ashtray, not even on the day he had given him his Zippo ...

"HAPPY BIRTHDAY, SON." *Dante slid a black box across his desk, toward him. "And congratulations."*

Lucca had just officially taken the underboss title. Now both the boss and underboss held the last name Caruso.

Not only was he the youngest to ever be made in the family, but now he held the title of becoming the youngest underboss in history, at the age of twenty-one. His father rarely showed he was proud of him, but today, he could clearly see it.

Opening the box, Lucca revealed the engraved, shiny silver Zippo he had seen his father use to light his cigars ever since he could remember. It was a family heirloom, a piece of Caruso history that had passed down through many generations.

He picked up the metal piece and flicked it open until the flame shone brightly. He was just as fascinated with it as he had been the first time he'd seen his father use it. It was the exact thing that had led to his fascination with fire. "Thank you."

"You're welcome. Now, why don't we light up some cigars to celebrate?" Dante eagerly went to his cigar box. He opened it, picked one up, and ran the thick cigar under his nose, smelling it, before he handed it to his son.

"No, thanks." Lucca shook his head, pulling out his pack of cigarettes. He took out the matches that read, "Kansas City Hotel" and threw them on the desk, no longer needing them. Then he placed a stick in his mouth. "I've got my own."

The pride on his father's face dropped the moment he used his Zippo for the first time on a cigarette and the smell began to fill his office.

Like Lucca had never developed a taste for cigars, Dante had never developed a taste for his son's smoke of choice, either. The only difference was Lucca never shamed him for it.

"Put that shit out." His father swatted the smoke away in a huff. "I've told you a million times not to smoke those in my office."

"Sorry." Lucca shrugged, clearly not sorry at all, and took one last puff before he leaned forward to put it out in his father's ashtray.

"Nuh-uh." Dante's tanned hand covered the crystal glass, stopping him. Sliding it closer to him, his father reminded him of a day that would be far, far into the future. "You can put your shit sticks out in this when I'm no longer the head of this family ..."

"Son ..."

Every hair on Lucca's body stood on end, knowing the day he had been waiting for had finally come.

"It's *time*."

A NEW ERA

Making an annotation to her notes, Chloe refused to become distracted by Adalyn typing in, *How much longer?* on her computer. With Adalyn's screen a centimeter away from hers, it would be hard to pretend she didn't see Adalyn's question.

Chloe pointed to the clock at the top right of the screen to remind her. *Ten minutes.*

Sassily, her friend deleted her earlier message to type, *Killlll meeee.*

She returned her attention to the professor, trying her best to ignore the sigh of irritation coming from directly beside her.

Typing in more notes, she somehow was able to become engrossed in the lecture even with the distraction.

The big wooden podium that sat in the front of the room kept the professor mostly there during his lectures, but every now and then, he'd walk toward the rows of students observing him, like he was doing now.

"Make sure you complete the questions 1, 5, and 6 in the review section at the end of the chapter. I expect the homework assignment to be completed by class tomorrow." Dismissing the class, he went back to the podium stand to shuffle through his notes.

A finally free Adalyn took no time to complain, "I thought I was going to *die* of starvation before he would shut up."

Closing her computer to put it in her backpack, Chloe glanced at her like she was crazy. "We had McDonald's before class."

"Which was *nothing!*"

What the frick is she talking about?

"You had a *two* egg McMuffins and *two* hashbrowns."

"Yeah, but they forgot my hotcakes, remember?" she politely reminded her.

Heaving her backpack over her shoulder, Chloe had no flipping idea how her friend stayed so small. If she ate like her, she'd be on *My 600lb Life*. "You're going to have a heart attack before you're thirty."

As they walked out of their row of seats, Adalyn grabbed her arm when she would have walked to where the professor was talking to several of the students then gave her a hard side eye. "What are you doing?"

She glanced down at the arm that was now entwined with hers. The Chloe before Lucca would have jumped out of her grasp, but the *Chloe now* didn't attempt to shrug out of it. Even though it did tend to still feel weird to be touched by anyone but Lucca, she knew her friend didn't mean any harm by it, and with how loving her girlfriend group was, Chloe was beginning to get used to it.

"I-I was just going to ask him a question."

Adalyn held on to her tightly and walked her toward the door. "I'll help you figure it out after lunch."

Chloe's eyes rolled heavenward as she tried not to laugh. "And what chapter are we on?"

"Okay, Elle will be able to help. Satisfied?" Adalyn groaned at having to fully drag her closer to the door. "*Now,* can we go eat?"

Knowing she was never going to win a battle against Adalyn's stomach, nor anything else against her, for that matter, she meekly gave in. Elle had a later class of Professor Miller's; she could ask her to find out the answer then.

When they left the building, Chloe noticed her three bodyguards take up strategic spots around them as they walked.

"Don't forget to do his assignment," she warned, knowing Adalyn was notorious for forgetting. "He takes off ten points if it isn't in before class."

"Kill me," Adalyn groaned, bringing life to her earlier sentiment. "I don't know why I decided to take his class, anyway."

"Because you need Political Science to grad—"

"No, that's not it," Adalyn shushed her, trying to think. Then her expression cleared. "I remember. It was because I saw Professor Miller during registration and wondered if he spelled his name d-a-d-d-y."

One thing was for sure when she was with Adalyn—she never knew what the hell would come out of her friend's mouth next.

"You took his class because you think he's cute?"

Adalyn's mouth practically fell to floor, appalled. "Are you not listening? There is nothing *cute* about Professor Miller. He's *gorgeous.*"

"Does Angel know you think Professor Miller is gorgeous?"

"No ... and you're not going to let it slip to Elle, either."

"I wouldn't have ..." Chloe looked at Adalyn to see the implied, almost harmless threat and decided to tease her more, anyway. "But why *shouldn't* I?"

Her friend had no trouble teasing her right back. "Because I would let it slip back that he spends most of the time staring at you."

Chloe's stomach started to churn nervously. "He doesn't."

"Yes, he does. You might not notice because you're staring at your computer"—she wiggled her brows mischievously—"*but I do.*"

She tried her best to nervously laugh it off. "Then you should start paying more attention to yours and not what I'm doing before you flunk out of class."

"I'm not going to flunk out." Adalyn didn't take offense. Her arm that was still entwined with hers pulled her in closer. "Professor Miller wouldn't flunk the best friend of the object of his fixation."

If he was staring at her, she knew exactly why—the same reason everyone else did.

Her scars.

It was Lucca's first official day. His father was in Cancun with Nadia and Leo by now, and he was relishing having full control. *Finally.*

A knock on the door had him leaning back in his chair. *Well, almost.*

"Come in."

A proud Vinny walked in through the door. "Congratulations," he greeted with a slow smile as he held out his hand, "boss."

"Thanks," Lucca said, taking his hand in a firm grip to shake it. It wasn't that Vinny Vitale was a bad consigliere. He was just his *father's* consigliere, and having Vinny around would always feel as if Dante were still around.

Dante, Enzo, and Vinny were all friends since birth, much like their sons, Nero, Amo, and Vincent. But Lucca didn't have any plans to make Vincent his consigliere ...

"Well, firstly"—the consigliere wasted no time taking a seat and getting straight to business—"have you come to a decision who your underboss will be?"

He already needed a fucking cigarette. Normally, Lucca wouldn't give a fuck and light up, but he was trying to show respect to his consigliere, and Vinny was like his father where cigars and cigarettes were concerned.

"I'm still considering my options."

"I see," Vinny drawled out as he adjusted himself more regally on the chair. The presence of excellence he always had just oozed out of him. There was no doubt who the best dressed in the family was. His suits easily cost in the thousands, and not only that, they were never repeated. Today, he sported a black suit with white pinstripes and a bloodred tie with a silk pocket square to match. He was definitely the most colorful of the family, with the most old-school look, as the pocket watch chain detail set him above the rest. It was a nice touch that always completed his look that he had yet to leave behind. "As you know, Enzo held the title until you came of age and would probably be the best fit for the next two years until Nero turns twenty-one."

Figures. He knew exactly what Vinny's opinion on the matter would be before he had even spoken it. Unfortunately for Lucca, he still had to at least listen to it. A consigliere's job was to consult the boss, and while Vinny was his equal in the Caruso family hierarchy, he held no real power. The only power he could hold was the weight of his words, and with the way Lucca worked, it was little. If there was something Lucca wanted to do, he would do it and ask for forgiveness later. Not that it ever came to that.

"Like I said"—deciding to fuck it, he placed a cigarette between his lips—"I'm still considering my options."

"Of course." Vinny's tone held the perfect amount of disinterest, like a consigliere pro. "As you should."

Lucca flicked open his Zippo to light the end of his precious cigarette, desperately wishing his sister were sitting in front of him already.

Unlike Vinny, his sister's mind worked a lot like his. It was in Maria's nature to want a crown and throne for herself. Instead, she had to sit there and watch Lucca have all the power given to him because she had not only been born a woman but second born.

Lucca himself knew that it was a shitty rule that should have died generations ago, because the throne should go to the most deserving person. It not only was the smartest decision, but it would always be best for the family. And what was best for the Caruso family now was to get rid of the old ways as a new era dawned.

"As the new head of the family, you are allowed to call in your *own* choice for consigliere, as well ..." Vinny had spoken as if they weren't discussing his own future, but he finally let it drop for just a moment to vouch for himself. "Although, I'm sure I have a few more years left in me before I must retire. I could hold out until Vincent comes of age, if it would make it easier for you."

Like the boss and underboss, where a man with the last name Caruso held the titles for generations, a Vitale held the consigliere position for the same span. So, having Maria stop that succession, along with being a woman, was going to go about as well as Humpty Dumpty being in an MMA fight.

However, it sadly was the *easiest* option for him at the moment. To change the old ways of the family would have to be done slowly. Lucca was going to have to choose the battles he wanted to fight one at a time while he transitioned into being the head of this family, and his first battle had already been chosen the moment he had slid that ring over Chloe's finger. The boss marrying a woman without a single trace of Italian blood was going to go as well as trying to convince Conor McGreggor to put Humpty Dumpty back together again.

Vinny's disinterested tone returned. "But, of course, it's entirely your choice, Lucca. Myself and the rest of the family will support you in whomever you choose."

That, he seriously doubted.

Nonetheless, Maria becoming consigliere was going to have to wait, and unfortunately for Lucca, he was going to have to deal with Vinny for a while longer.

"I see no need to change the family dynamics at this point in time." While it wasn't the complete truth, it also wasn't a total lie, as he didn't want to go there at the moment. Right now, only one thing mattered. "I think it's best to handle the threat to our family before I make any decisions."

"I think that's wise," Vinny agreed.

Taking a long draw, Lucca started to relax after buying himself some time before needing to name an underboss.

Suddenly, Vinny's face turned haughty at the thought of the person who was destroying the family as he continued, "Are you any closer to finding out who One-Shot is?"

"Sooner or later, they will make a mistake." Lucca's eyes

glowed as brightly as the end of his cigarette. "He's good, but he's starting to lose control ... I know it."

Vinny raised a curious brow. "How do you know?"

"His attempt on my father's life with the car was erratic. He's no longer precise, and I think it's because of his last failed attempts. My guess is his next hit will be the biggest failure of them all and may very well cost him his identity." Lucca smashed the butt of his cigarette into the crystal ashtray. "If there's one thing I know, it's that One-Shot should go back to the Glock."

"Yes, I think you're right about that. We can only hope the next mistake he makes *is grave.*" Vinny nodded in agreement before getting up. "Well, if there's nothing else you'd like to discuss, I must be go—"

"Actually," Lucca stopped him, "there is a matter I'd like to speak to you about."

Vinny clearly hadn't expected that as he took back the chair. "My time is yours."

Lucca found it hard to finally find the words for the thing he had wanted for so long, so he just came out with it. "I'd like to marry Chloe."

His consigliere had to clear his throat. "Well, I suppose I expected this to come up eventually."

"And with your experience, I'm hoping you could come up with a plan to best handle this situation, as it will not only benefit Dante's sons but your son, as well," Lucca stated, reminding him Vincent was currently dating a girl who didn't hold a drop of Italian blood, either.

"Right, well, Vincent isn't engaged to be wed, and let's hope he won't be anytime soon." Vinny secretly admitted strictly between the two, "But I'd probably say the best course of action would be to wait for Nero and Vincent to take their rightful positions in a few years, and then *the rest* of the family will simply follow *the heads* of the family." Smiling, he held up three long fingers. "I've always found three is better than one."

While his consigliere had a point, there was no way in hell Lucca was waiting that long to marry Chloe, even if he was to appoint Vincent as his equal. But there was no fucking way in hell that was happening, either.

"Let me reiterate." Lucca cleared his own throat, making sure he could be heard. "I *will* be marrying Chloe ... *next month.*"

"Ah." Vinny adjusted his expensive Italian jacket before smoothing down his dirty-blond hair that was slowly going gray. "Now I understand."

"Exactly." Lucca was glad he had gotten the message, but now he needed to butter his consigliere up in hopes it could encourage his cooperation. To have Vinny's approval of his and Chloe's marriage would go a long way with his men who lived and died by the old ways. "If anyone knows how to handle this matter best, it would be you."

Vinny thought hard about how to respond for a few moments. "Right, well—"

Beep, beep.

The sound of the fire alarm going off had both men jumping to their feet. It was only a second later that the office door flung open.

What the—

Sal officially put an end to their meeting. "Fire."

UMW: ULTIMATE MAFIA WIFE

"He is *not* fixated on me."

Adalyn made a shushing noise. "Careful, or they will hear what we're arguing about."

Noticing one of her bodyguards had moved closer and within hearing distance, they changed the subject to dress fittings for the bridesmaids as they arrived at the food court at the same time as Elle.

"What are you getting?" she asked her best friend with a smile.

Elle smiled even brighter at seeing her. "Chicken sandwich and chips. How about you?"

"A yogurt. We had McDonald's before class."

Chloe and Elle were sure to let Adalyn go first.

"Did Adalyn not get McDonald's?" her best friend asked, listening to the huge order she gave.

Violently, she nodded her head.

"Then why—"

"They forgot her hotcakes," Chloe whispered into her ear.

Elle nodded, understanding now. "That's the worst."

"Tomorrow, I'm going to suggest Burger King." She could already picture the scene that would await McDonald's drive-through window in the morning if they were to go there.

"If you're going to get her away from those golden arches, you need to come up with a place better than Burger King." Elle laughed. "But good luck with that. You won't be able to help yourself when she starts pouting for her Mickeydee's."

Chloe's shoulders slumped. Elle was right; she was a pushover. It was one of her many failings.

Noticing the sudden change in her best friend, Elle nudged her. "Hey, what's that look for?"

"Nothing." She tried shrugging it off.

Giving her a disbelieving glance, she moved forward to give her order before Chloe did the same. "You can grab us a table while we get our drinks."

"Okay," she agreed, taking the number stand from Elle.

Finding a seat in the busy food court wasn't easy. She was beginning to think they would have to take the food to go when one of the bodyguards motioned for her. Two guys were shoving the last of their sandwiches into their mouths as she approached.

"Y-you don't have to leave ..." Chloe began, wanting to ease their frightened expressions.

"We were done," one of them said, trying to rush. "We have class."

Chloe didn't believe him for a second and was going to say something to the bodyguard, but her friends' arrival with the drinks stopped her. She would have to take it up with Lucca later.

"Are you getting excited about going wedding dress shopping?" Elle asked once they were settled.

"When is it?" Adalyn asked.

Chloe started to reach forward to take the double burger away from her. "Greasy food is warping your mind."

"I was just kidding. I know when it is." Adalyn defended her burger protectively. "You take everything so seriously lately."

Staring down at her yogurt glumly, she had to admit that Adalyn was right. The day Lucca's father told him he would be taking over the family business, Lucca had come home that night and told her he wanted to marry her in a month. Next thing she knew, Maria had walked through the door to begin planning with her. Everything since, in the last few days, had been a blur.

It wasn't that Chloe didn't want to marry Lucca, because she definitely did. She just didn't understand the big hurry to get it done by next month and how the Carusos could manage to pull off a wedding in a month blew her mind every time she thought of it.

"Cut it out, Adalyn," Elle butted in politely. "Chloe just wants the wedding to go smoothly."

"How couldn't it? She has you, Maria, Kat, Lake, and me helping her. It's going to be the biggest wedding the city has ever seen."

Chloe finally lost what appetite she had left and pushed her yogurt away.

"Adalyn! You're not helping." Elle's politeness had worn thin. "Chloe is nervous enough without you making it worse."

"It's all right, Elle. I wasn't hungry, anyway."

Feeling bad, Adalyn pushed the yogurt back. "Eat. I won't say anything else."

Both Elle and she looked at Adalyn in disbelief.

"Okay, I'll *try* not to say anything else," she corrected.

Chloe didn't start eating again until Adalyn started making a dent in the huge amount of food she had ordered. Luckily, Elle sensed her tension and started chatting about their political science classes.

Taking out her computer and notebook, she showed Elle the question she had wanted to ask the professor. "After your class, could you ask him this?"

"Sure, but why didn't you just ask him yourself?"

"Adalyn was afraid all the hamburgers would sell out before she could get here."

"I see." Elle busted out in laughter. "I don't mind. I usually come up with a question to talk to him about, anyway. This saves me the trouble. I want it to be hard enough he'll think I'm smart enough to ask it, but not so hard I can't understand his answer."

Confused as to why Elle would bother putting in so much thought for a question to ask, Chloe stared at her friend. "Why?"

Elle raised her eyebrows so high they looked like one line. "Are you kidding? He's—"

"Gorgeous," Adalyn filled in for her after a big swallow.

"I was going to say hot, but he's that, too."

"Seriously?" Chloe looked at her in disbelief, beginning to feel as if she was missing something about the professor's appeal. "You, too?"

"Yes." Elle gave her a strange look. "Me and most of the students who go here. You don't find him attractive?"

"Find who attractive?" Lake asked, finally able to join up with them as she placed down her own food.

"Professor Miller," both Elle and Adalyn said in unison.

"Oh yeah, he's hot," Lake easily agreed.

Chloe decided to state the obvious that all her friends were clearly missing, "Um, he's our professor."

"So? That doesn't mean I don't have two eyes in my head, nor that I would ever cheat on Vincent, but ... I can still appreciate how fine he is," Lake said, opening her salad.

"Well, I don't," Chloe said simply.

The three girls looked at her as if she had sprouted two heads. Then Adalyn made all of them jump when she suddenly snapped her fingers, coming to a conclusion.

"I know why you don't find him attractive. It's because of Lucca."

Huh?

"What does Lucca have to do with it?"

Adalyn wagged her eyebrows at her again. "Because he's finer than the professor."

"Ah ..." Elle sighed. "That makes total sense. Lucca is more attractive."

"If that's the truth, I don't see you guys trying to get Lucca's attention when we hang out together."

Her friends stared at each other before turning to stare at her.

Lake asked, "You going to tell her, or should I?"

"I will," Elle replied, setting down her sandwich to focus on her words. "Other than we love our men and would do nothing to jeopardize our relationship with them, neither Lake nor I would ever flirt with Lucca. He's too scary."

"Yeah, and I wouldn't flirt with him *anymore* ..." Adalyn interjected, making herself clear. Being a mafia wife had been her dream, and Lucca being the boss would have made her a UMW: Ultimate Mafia Wife. But ever since he'd met Chloe and she'd met Angel, she was more than happy of not becoming a UME, of course.

"Lucca isn't scary." Chloe couldn't believe this blas—

"Scary like Zac Efron playing Ted Bundy scary," Elle told her gently.

"Oh, I have better than that ..." Adalyn bounced in her chair. "Skeet Ulrich in *Scream* scary."

"That's a good one," Lake agreed while Adalyn tried to keep her swooning to a minimum. "I can definitely see the resemblance there."

Chloe was shocked by her friends' view of her fiancé, so much so she felt the need to defend him. "Lucca isn't a serial killer."

"We aren't saying that, per se ..." Elle made at a face at Adalyn when she started eating again to avoid her eyes. "We're just saying he puts off the attitude he *could* be."

"Wow ..." An appalled Chloe looked each one of her girlfriends in the eyes before she moved on to the next. "I didn't know you thought that about Lucca."

Adalyn rolled her eyes upward. "Oh, come on, Chloe; you have to admit Lucca is kinda scary."

"He isn't to m—"

Lake raised a brow this time. "Be truthful, Chloe ... you weren't ever afraid of Lucca?"

Chloe had to think back for a moment. It seemed like an eternity since she had woken up in his bedr—

Oh ... Nervously, she bit her lip. *Well, shit.*

BACK TO THE OLD WAYS

Lucca stared at the black soot beneath his feet. His first day on the job had gone up in flames, *literally*. The only reason he had kept his sanity up until this point was because he knew Chloe was safe at school.

"Thankfully, the firefighters were able to put it out before it reached the Casino Hotel." It was clear Sal tried to look on the bright side. "But the diner will need to be demo'ed."

"And the cause?" Vinny asked the question that was on everyone's mind.

Sal shoved his hands in his trouser pockets and rocked. "Don't know yet, but by the looks of it ... arson."

Crouching, Lucca picked up some of the ashes, letting them run through his fingers. "One-Shot did this."

"Are you sure?" Vinny asked.

He nodded confidently. "Certain of it."

"I think so, too," Sal agreed. "The diner was one of the first businesses your father placed under his protection. I don't think it's a coincidence that, on your first day of taking over, this place gets hit. One-Shot is sending you a message."

Lucca stood defiantly, making a promise and wishing that fucker were here to hear it. "Well, I plan on answering it."

Brring.

Vinny's phone ringing had him retrieving it from his pocket. "I need to take this, but I'll think about how to best handle the matter we discussed," he promised before stepping away as Lucca gave him an appreciative nod.

It wasn't until their consigliere left that Sal's mood changed. "I've tried everything to figure out who he is, Lucca. I don't know how he's keeping himself hidden from me ..." He spoke as if he was talking to a friend and not his boss. "But he is."

Lucca didn't miss the disappointment in his voice, knowing The Great Salvatore's pride was on the line, but he didn't doubt Sal's ability for a second. There was something he was missing, and it was probably staring them all right in the face ...

As he scanned the scene for a few more minutes in silence, it reminded him of hell.

"Maybe the reason you can't find him"—the wheels began turning in Lucca's mind—"is the exact reason you're never going to find him from behind your computer screen."

Sal stared at him as if Lucca had inhaled too much smoke. "Huh?"

Finally, he had his first clue. "He's old-school."

"Well, then he's definitely not from this era if I can't find him," Sal stated, his mood beginning to improve at the thought he wasn't so bad after all. "So, what do we do?"

"We go back to the old ways," Lucca replied, knowing that was the exact thing he was trying to get away from. But, in some respects, the way they had handled business back then *was timeless*. "But first, I need to talk to someone I haven't yet about this who's from that era."

And tonight, he was going to pay him a visit.

Sal's brows furrowed. "Who?"

"The devil."

CHLOE ENTERED the penthouse suite with the light tinge of smoke from the diner clinging to the air. The reason it didn't bother her much was because she could still smell the delicious aromas coming from the kitchen.

She hung up her backpack in the closet; she would retrieve it when Lucca did his rounds in the casino after dinner. He was usually gone for a couple of hours, giving her the opportunity to do her homework while he worked.

Walking up next to Lucca, she pressed a kiss to his waiting mouth. "Sorry about the diner."

"Don't worry about it, darlin'." Lucca picked up his wine glass from the counter and took a rather long sip.

Knowing he didn't want to talk about it, she changed the subject with a smile. "What are we having for dinner?"

"Chicken parmesan." Stirring the sauce in the pan, he continued, "How were classes?"

"Fine." She went to steal a small sip from his glass. "Same as usual."

Lifting the glass back to his lips before she could grab it, he downed the rest of the contents and began filling it up again from the open bottle that sat on the counter. "Henry said he thought he heard you and Adalyn arguing on the way to lunch?"

Chloe's eyes suddenly darted down to the dark color of

the wine. "It wasn't a big deal. I don't even know why Henry would mention that to you in the first place."

Lucca's blue-green gaze began studying her. "He said you seemed upset."

"Well, *I* was more upset when he made two students choke their meal down so they could give us their table." Chloe looked him in the eyes now, hoping it was somewhat defiantly. "Did he mention that to you, too?"

"Yes, he did, as a matter of fact."

Noticing he wasn't the least bit sympathetic, she started stepping away from the counter. "I'm going to get changed."

Lucca, however, grabbed her wrist before she could leave. "Go ahead. Dinner will be done in ten minutes. But, Chloe?" He brought her closer so he could lower his mouth to her ear. "Don't think I didn't notice you changed the subject from Adalyn."

When his grasp left her, she was able to finally go upstairs to change into more comfortable clothes before coming back down to see Lucca had already set the food on the table and was waiting for her.

The silence as they ate made the food hard to swallow, so she gave in, deciding to break it. "Adalyn and I were arguing over if the professor stares at me during class."

Lucca neatly cut a piece of the chicken with his knife. "Is he?"

"No." At least, she didn't think so ...

He took another bite. "Adalyn comes across to me as *very* observant where men are concerned."

Damn. Honestly, he had her there.

"He pays no more attention to me than any other student in the class."

"*That*, I don't believe." At her anxious glance, Lucca gave her a comforting smile as he began swirling the wine in his glass around and around. "Why are you looking so worried, darlin'? I can't say I blame the man."

Chloe's anxiousness grew worse as he continued. She hadn't quite seen Lucca like this before ...

"Has Adalyn got you watching too many *Godfather* movies? If I promise not to *whack* him, will you finish your dinner? Henry mentioned you didn't eat much at lunch."

"Lucca!" Chloe dropped her utensils; they made a loud clinking sound. "They don't need to watch me every second then report it back to you. Don't you think it's becoming too much? I've started to make sure one of them doesn't follow me in the restroom when I need to go on campus."

"I'll tell them to tone it down. I wasn't aware they were making you feel uncomfortable." He gave her an apologetic smile.

Chloe smiled back, showing him she didn't blame him.

Elle, Adalyn, and Lake were *so* wrong about Lucca. He was the kindest fiancé and wanted nothing more than to make her happy and safe. All she had to do was communicate her feelings, and he would move heaven and earth to make her happy. How damn lucky could she be?

Now, if she could learn how to be more like Maria, she'd have it made.

Hmm, maybe with a little help, she could have it all? And she knew just the person to call ...

TAKING DOWN THE PATRIARCHY

O pening the door to a tall, six-foot, legged blonde brought a smile to her face. "Thanks for coming so soon."

"No problem." Maria flipped her blonde locks, letting her know it was nothing. "I needed to go over more wedding stuff with you, anyway."

"O-oh, great ..." Unable to hide her lack of enthusiasm, Chloe at least was grateful she'd have an excuse of why Maria stopped by so late if Lucca came back.

Her future sister-in-law eyed her up and down as she tapped the toe of her stiletto on the floor. "What's wrong?"

"Nothing." Immediately, regret filled her. She wasn't so sure she could ask her anymore. All she could hope for now was to deflect and pray she'd be too busy talking about wedding stuff. "How are you able to still walk in heels pregnant?"

Chloe was always amazed how Maria could defy gravity in her tall stilettos, but doing that pregnant was a different feat altogether. It wasn't only her heels that had her in awe, but it was also the fact she still fit in her wardrobe of short dresses. Maria somehow looked even more beautiful in them with her growing bump that appeared like a little basketball was hiding under the expensive fabric.

"Honey, not even my firstborn child could keep me away from my Louboutins." Making herself at home, Maria took a seat on the couch and placed her hand on her belly. "Now, tell me what's wrong and why I'm here."

Honestly, Chloe should have known better. There was no getting anything past Maria.

"I wanted to ask you a personal question."

"Anything," the beautiful blonde said, eager to help in any way she could. If there was one thing she loved about Maria, it was that she was a girl's girl.

"With whom your father and brother are, and all of their men around you every day," she began, trying to find the words as she looked down at her feet, "how are you …?"

Maria arched a brow, trying to help her out. "Sane?"

"Well, that, too." She chuckled. "But how are you *you?*"

With the mafia princess being a lot of things, she wasn't quite sure what part of her she was talking about.

"Like, how did you learn to stand up for yourself and be so confident?" Chloe finally managed to come out with the reason why she had asked her here in the first place.

"Well, for starters"—with Maria now understanding why she was here, her sweet voice took a tone that reminded Chloe of her professors—"I learned to always look everyone in the eye."

Her gray eyes slowly lifted up to the emerald-green ones that reminded her of the green in Lucca's.

"Eye contact always shows that you're confident enough in yourself to look them in the eye. You never want to look away first; you always want them to. And *especially* if it's a man," her future sister-in-law began coaching her encouragingly.

"Okay." As confidently as she could, Chloe nodded. "I'll try my best."

"*Oh Lord,*" Maria mumbled as her beautiful face fell, but before Chloe could ask what was wrong, she answered, "We're going to be here for a while."

LUCCA SAT in the metal chair, watching the grotesque thing eat his way back to manhood until the creature finally returned to the land of the living.

"Two meals so close together ..." Lucifer wiped the stains from his mouth. "Something's happened on the outside, hasn't it?"

There was one thing Lucifer never was, and that was *stupid.*

Lucca flexed his jaw, regretting coming here the other day to brag that he had been made king.

"Let's play a game." Lucifer laughed, leaning his back against the wall where he sat on the cold, dirty floor. "I try to guess, and you tell me when I get it right."

Squeezing his fists, he had to remind himself that Lucifer would always try to bait him so he would finally kill him. Unfortunately for Lucca, with the state the devil was in after being in here for so long, it meant anything could kill him at this point.

"Let's see ... you made a mistake?" Lucifer began guessing but then shook his head. "No, that's not it. *Lucca Caruso* would never make a mistake."

So far, Lucca wasn't liking this game.

"Hmm ... Could it be being the boss isn't what you

thought it'd be? Nope, that's not it, either." Lucifer's black orbs met his. "We both know that sitting on the throne is everything we ever wanted."

Getting annoyed, he was about to tell him to shut the fuck up already.

"Oh, I know. Kansas City has a serial killer on the loose!" Lucifer roared with laughter like a hyena, but then his laughter died. It was obvious he had only been joking to annoy his captor, but then he realized it might not be a joke after all when he noticed Lucca's fists tighten. "Is there?"

Lucca leaned back in his chair and crossed his arms.

"There is." A sinister smile lifted Lucifer's lips. "Let me guess, he's not terrorizing the city; he's terrorizing *you*."

His blue-green gaze pierced the devil's. "How'd you know?"

"Good guess, I suppos—"

When Lucca jumped out of his chair and toward him, Lucifer cowered, trying to protect himself.

"It's obvious!"

Lucca suddenly stopped mere inches away.

"When you take someone out of the game"—his dirty palm hit his own chest, signaling himself—"two more will eventually pop up." That, he did know. It was why he had his son sitting next to him on the throne.

When Lucca took back his seat, Lucifer relaxed again.

"I may have been a strong player in the game, but there's always someone better waiting in the shadows to take your place."

Lucca knew exactly what he meant by those words. "Like how I replaced you?"

"Yes." Lucifer seemed to rather hate admitting it, but the chains holding him in this cell were a constant reminder of that fact. "But you'd do well to remember what I just said."

The devil's friendly warning hadn't fallen on deaf ears. In fact, it was something that kept Lucca up at night. "Oh, I know. I figured that out at eighteen."

"You know when I figured it out?" Lucifer's voice went grave. "The second you dragged that rat inside the restaurant the day you were made. I secretly knew then I didn't have a chance against you, even though I didn't want to admit it."

Lucca actually laughed. "And do you know who gave me my revelation?"

Lucifer went silent as he thought for a moment before he proudly smiled. "I'm guessing one of my boys."

"Cassius."

"Ha!" Lucifer bellowed with laughter. "Sounds about right."

Yes, if there was one thing about the mafia world, karma was a sick bitch.

Holding his stomach, Lucifer stopped laughing from the pain, and that was when it started to click. "If you were eighteen, that would mean ... How did you know so young?"

Lucca didn't hide his disappointment. "And you didn't?"

"Truthfully," Lucifer seemed to reminisce in sadness, "I knew I wasn't going to last by the time he got old enough. I had my best one too old."

He didn't give the devil the satisfaction in knowing that the making of his first creation would have been the only one possible to take him out. He had gotten a hold of Cassius young enough, but Dominic ... he hadn't known his true potential until it was too late. But thankfully, none of that mattered anymore since the families had mixed.

Lucca was here for a different reason.

Taking out a cigarette, he flipped open his Zippo, casting an orange glow over the damp, dark room. "We call him One-Shot." Taking a long hit before continuing, he touched the space between his eyes. "In the beginning, every man he killed was shot by putting a bullet right here."

Lucifer's soulless eyes grew big.

"And I know what you're thinking." Lucca exhaled a cloud of smoke. "It's not Dom; trust me. All the bullets entered through the back of the head."

His eyes returning to normal size, he agreed. "'Cause I taught my son you should always let them know a Luciano was the one to send you to hell."

Lucca had figured as much.

As he continued smoking his cigarette, he told his enemy in chains everything Lucifer had missed about One-Shot while he had sat in this cell. It was apparent Lucifer loved hearing about everything he missed on the outside, too.

"And I know it was him who started that fire."

"Oh, it was." Lucifer nodded with a smile. "I would have probably done the same fucking thing on your first day."

"I don't fucking doubt it ..." Lucca's voice trailed off as he realized something. It wasn't hearing about the outside world that was making his captor happy; it was—

"You know who it is." It wasn't a question but a statement.

Lucifer's maniacal laughter bounced off the walls as if, suddenly, hundreds of devils were surrounding him at once. "And you don't?"

"No one. Not one person out there knows who it is."

Lucca pointed to the big metal sliding door before he slowly pointed to Lucifer. "But you're telling me you do?"

"Oh, I do," he promised. Instinctively, Lucca knew it to be true.

He stood suddenly, causing Lucifer to cower in the corner, but this time, Lucca grabbed the chain that was connected to his ankle and pulled it closer to him. The chain rattled as he dragged the creature out of the corner and to his feet.

Crouching down, he grabbed its face, squeezing the life out of it in the palm of his hand. "Who *is it*?"

Lucifer could barely speak out of his smushed-up mouth. "If I tell you, I'm left alive. But if I don't ..."

"Then I might kill you in the process," Lucca gritted through his teeth.

Sadly, there wasn't much left of Lucifer these days, so he was right—the defiance in his black eyes told him he would hold on to the name so he could finally meet his death, but Lucca had made a promise to keep his vessel here, so his soul could stay on earth for a little while longer.

He still held his face tightly, contemplating what to do. *To kill or not to kill* that was the question until, finally, he let his face go.

"What?" Lucifer cried, still wishing for death. Then, when he watched Lucca begin to leave, he was desperate enough to try a different tactic. "You'll come back when One-Shot finally comes for your precious Chlo—"

Her full name hadn't even left his mouth when Lucca grabbed his face again. Except, this time, he slid his long fingers inside his mouth and down his throat, forcing the precious food and nutrients he had just given his frail body up.

"I should thank you." Satisfied, Lucca dropped his face

until it dropped into his own filth. "You just helped me discover how to bring One-Shot into the light."

This time as Lucca left, nothing Lucifer said, no matter how much the devil baited him, turned him back.

Lucifer knowing who it was proved something, and it no longer mattered if he told him or not.

And you don't? His words followed by his maniacal laughter rang through his head, but Lucifer had made a mistake in telling him that.

One-Shot's identity must not only be so obvious that he was overlooking it ...

But their paths must cross *every day*.

By the time Maria got up to leave, Chloe was already feeling like a brand-new woman. "Seriously, Maria, I can't thank you enough for everyth—"

"Pshht, please," the tall, legged blonde shushed her. "If there's anything I live for, it's weddings and taking down the patriarchy."

Chloe smiled, knowing there was never a truer statement Maria had made.

"Now remember, if you find yourself getting nervous"— she held up a slender finger—"just think WWMD."

"Got it." She nodded studiously, remembering that part of her lecture. She already started practicing.

WWMD, WWM—

"Oh, and Chloe ..." Maria smiled a little too sweetly. "If Lucca isn't treating you right, I can always get Dom to kill him."

THE VILLAGE IDIOT

"You get your assignment in on time?" Chloe asked as she was taking her computer out of her backpack. Busy perching her computer closer to where she was about to place it, a surprised Adalyn looked at her. "What assignment?"

"The questions the professor assigned to us yesterday. *The ones I told you not to forget,*" Chloe tried jogging her memory, but if it was nothing worth remembering to Adalyn, who was practically a goldfish.

"I forgot." Turning on her computer, Adalyn played it off like it was no big deal. "It'll give me something to do during class, anyway."

"He's going to take off ten points because it's late," Chloe reminded her.

"Not if one of my besties goes up and tells him I needed to take my grandmother to the ER, and I had to leave her deathbed to come to class."

This time when she looked at her like she was crazy, at least it was deserving. "You're joking?"

"No. I need this class, and I don't want to take it over," Adalyn whined. "And especially not without you."

"Then try taking it more seriously," Chloe tried departing her wisdom but felt bad if it was possibly true ... "Is your grandmother still alive?"

"No."

When Chloe looked as if she was about to cry, Adalyn waved her hand. "But she's been dead for years."

Chloe came to the conclusion right there that Adalyn lived in her own world, *and the rest of us are just participants*.

"I'm not lying to Professor Miller."

"Then don't. I will." She shrugged. "Just don't expect me to lie for *you* when you miss an assignment."

I'll take my chances.

Glancing toward the doorway, Chloe saw the professor's TA enter the room.

"I'll be giving Professor Miller's lesson today," the TA told them.

Chloe ignored Adalyn's ecstatic expression as the lecture began, knowing the TA didn't dock points off their homework for turning it in after class.

A spark of suspicion started to worry her until she told herself it wasn't the first time the TA had taken over for the professor.

Once their lecture came to an end, Chloe glanced around, and when she couldn't spot any of her security guards, any remaining suspicion died.

"The place is packed today," Elle commented, coming to stand with her as they waited for a table to open.

Both Adalyn's mouth and stomach groaned. "It's going to take forever to get a table."

A big smile on her face, Chloe nodded happily. "Isn't it

great!"

Elle pressed the back of her hand to Chloe's forehead. "Are you sick?"

"No." She swatted it away. "I told Lucca my guards were watching me too closely, so he promised to make them give me space."

"You couldn't have told him to make an exception for lunch?" Adalyn mumbled.

"No, Chloe is right," Elle spoke up, taking her side. "I'd rather wait if it makes her more comfortable."

"I suppose," Adalyn mumbled even lower this time.

"You can sit here. I'm almost finished," a girl called out, attracting their attention. Neither Adalyn nor Elle had to be told twice.

"Thank you," Chloe told her, not recognizing her from any of her classes.

"No biggie. My classes don't start until twelve, so I always try to get here earlier than the lunch crowd."

Adalyn nudged her. "I told you we should have taken later classes."

"You didn't have to take the morning class with me. You could have taken the later one with Elle." It was only her and Elle's schedules that contradicted due to their majors, but hell, at this point, Chloe would have preferred attending the class solo.

"Oh yes, I did. I need to pass, and no offense"—Adalyn looked at Elle—"but they're not as smart as you. And, in order for *me* to pass, I need a *genius*."

"None taken." Elle chuckled.

It was Adalyn who finally introduced themselves to the girl who had invited them to share the table. "I'm Adalyn. This is Chloe and Elle."

"And I'm Lake." The tall brunette joined them, late as

usual. Leave it to Vincent to always make her late.

"Nice to meet you all. I'm Gia." Standing up with her tray to grab the backpack hanging on the chair, she gave them all a hurried smile. "It's nice to meet you all. See you around."

Opening her salad, Chloe grimaced at the wilted leaves. "I should have stuck with the yogurt."

"Lesson learned." Elle frowned, looking at it. "Stick to what you can see before you order."

"I will. By the way"—Chloe closed the salad, unable to bring herself to eat it—"don't expect Professor Miller to be in class today. His TA gave his class this morning."

"There is a God." Elle looked upward as she clasped her hands together. "I forgot to do my assignment, so now I can do it during the lecture."

"Oh gosh, not you, too ..." Chloe groaned, seeing that Adalyn was rubbing off on her best friend.

Knowing exactly what she was thinking, Adalyn gave her a pitying look. "Do you ever do anything fun lately?"

Chloe bit her lip, trying to think of the last fun thing she had done. Truthfully, between her bodyguards watching her every move and the wedding planning, she hadn't had much as of late, so she lied. "I have fun all the time ..."

Even Elle gave her a doubting look at that.

"I do." *Lies.*

Adalyn popped a fry into her mouth. "Chloe, working in your greenhouse shouldn't be considered fun at your age."

Oh, shit, she had forgotten about that. That was fun, *right?* "Why not, if that's how I enjoy spending my time?"

"So, you don't want to come over to mine and Angel's place to watch a movie tonight?"

"I'll watch the movie," Chloe conceded only when Elle

nodded her head that she was in, too. "*After* I do my homework."

"Hear that, Elle?" Adalyn happily popped another fry into her mouth. "She's going to watch a movie with us."

"I'll bring the popcorn." There was nothing Elle loved more than a good movie night.

"I'll bring the candy!" Lake grinned unabashedly at inviting herself over. "We need to ask Kat and Maria, though. We don't want them to feel left out."

Chloe resignedly knew when she had been set up. "The more—"

—*THE MERRIER*, Lucca had to remind himself when he let the village idiot come in. Even though he wanted to kill Vincent every now and again, he only let him enter because one thing was for sure ...

There was no fucking way in hell Vincent was One-Shot, and right now, Lucca needed all the help they could get. Even *if* it was that of an idiot.

As bad as it sounded, the poor thing wasn't smart enough to even be capable of it, not to mention too vain and busy looking at himself in the mirror to even bother. It was a wonder how he and his stepsister, Adalyn, weren't biologically related. Because, even though his fiancée would never say it, he knew there was no possible way her friend didn't drive Chloe up the wall being in class with her every day.

Looking around the room at Nero, Maria, Sal, Drago, Amo, Vincent, and Angel, he remembered the first time he'd gathered them all together what seemed like an eternity ago ...

. . .

"NOW THAT WE'RE ALL HERE"—LUCCA *flipped his lighter open to take a much-needed hit off a cigarette—"look around to the people in this room."*

Eyeing everyone in the room himself, he saw their faces turned serious; the boardroom they were in quickly turning into a war room with just a few words.

"These are the only faces you can trust," their underboss continued, commanding each and every one. "Anyone outside, we cannot trust isn't One-Shot. No matter who it is."

Solemnly, every soldier nodded their head, fully understanding that he was suspecting a Caruso to hide behind the curtain.

"One-Shot might be gone for now, but he will return ... and when he does, the only one who will deal with him"— looking at each pair of eyes, Lucca staked his claim—"is me."

LUCCA WASTED no time getting right to it. "One-Shot is one of us."

"One of us?" Vincent's baby blues darted around the room in shock until they stopped on Angel suspiciously. "Gee, I wonder which one of us is not like the other ..."

"Not us, you idiot." Grabbing the bridge of his nose was better than grabbing Vincent's neck as Lucca contemplated for the millionth time why he had let him in in the first place.

"A Caruso," Maria finished for him, stating the fucking obvious that everyone else knew.

"Oh, my bad." Vincent threw the Luciano an apologetic glance. "Old habits die hard."

The tatted angel didn't even bother. "Sure."

"Anyway, back to what I was saying." Lucca took back

command of the room. "I know we've all had our suspicions it might've been a Caruso all along, but I'm almost positive it is now."

It wasn't until Amo regretfully said, "I agree," that everyone else seemed convinced. When it came from a Caruso who had done some things he shouldn't have ... his insight was insurmountable.

"How?" his brother, Nero, asked with his green gaze turning into slits.

"When Dominic took over as head of the Luciano family, he wiped out Lucifer's followers, which were the older generation of family members."

"That's correct," Angel backed up the claim, knowing most of the Luciano men left weren't much older than Dom. "But what does that have to do with One-Shot's identity?"

Sal was the one to answer. "Because I can't find a single trace of him."

"So, we're left to believe he's a man with the love for the old ways," Lucca continued.

It was as if you could see the light bulb going off above everyone's head.

Drago cracked his knuckles, ready to break some necks. "What's the plan, then, *boss*?"

"We do what our fathers and their fathers did ..." He wanted to pull out a cigarette but settled for flipping his lighter when his sister gave him a death glare to remind him of her condition. "Go old-school."

"And *how* exactly do we do that?" Vincent asked, wondering if he was just too dumb, too young, or simply both in this case to understand.

Lucca flipped his silver Zippo to a close, capturing the flame. "We set a trap."

WWMD. WHAT WOULD MARIA DO.

Fortunately for them, they were able to tag team Gia for a table for the rest of the week. When Monday came and Professor Miller's TA continued to teach his class, Chloe's suspicions were aroused again.

By the end of the class, she knew exactly who was responsible.

"I'm going to miss lunch today. I need to run back to the penthouse. I forgot a paper I need for my next class. Can I borrow your car?" Thankfully, Lucca had let the girls drive lately as their guards followed closely behind.

Adalyn looked at her quizzically. "Why not have Lucca send someone with what you forgot or get Henry to drive you?"

By now, Chloe had taken a few lessons from Maria. Each time they went over wedding stuff, her future sister-in-law took the opportunity to sprinkle in her "How to Become a Badass Woman Overnight." She really thought Maria needed to write a book.

"Why ask someone else when I can do it myself?"

Not knowing what was coming over her friend, Adalyn

still wasn't convinced. "I don't want to get in trouble with Lucca."

"*Please*, Adalyn. You won't get in any trouble. *I promise.*"

At her promise, Adalyn handed her the keys. "I'm going to be dead meat, but go ahead. Just remember this the next time I need your help."

Knowing Adalyn, she'd definitely need her help one day, so she made her another promise. "The next time you resurrect your grandmother, just to bring her back to death's door, I'll even bring you flowers."

"Now, you don't have to go that far ..." However, she still liked her enthusiasm. "But if you could manage a few tears, that would be great."

"I'll be back before our next class." Chloe took off and wasted no time reaching the parked car they had left earlier this morning. She thought she had successfully dodged the suits who were supposed to appear invisible, so it wasn't until she pulled out that she noticed them racing for her.

She didn't even bother to try to lose them when they finally caught up to her on the drive back to the casino. She pulled up to the front of the hotel and threw the car in *park*, trying to pump herself up for what she was about to do.

WWMD. What Would Maria Do. WWMD.

Finally able to channel her inner Maria, she got out and threw the valet the key. "I'll be back in ten minutes. I want it here when I get back." As she mimicked the authoritative way Maria would talk to people, her confidence was given a much-needed boost at his respectful nod.

With her security beginning to catch up to her, she managed to jump through the rotating door without them, and as it spun, she gave Henry one of Maria's death glares through the glass.

"You can wait here," Chloe said, entering the elevator. However, only the door already sliding closed had given her the courage to say that to him.

When she punched in the secret code of buttons to take her straight to the top, Chloe felt a spurt of satisfaction at outsmarting them.

Ding.

The elevator door sliding open had Chloe at a standstill when Sal appeared to be waiting on the other side.

"Lucca is in his office. He's waiting for you."

"Perfect," she said and walked down the hall.

Any other time, Chloe would be hesitant to talk to Lucca when she had done something she probably shouldn't have, but today wasn't that day.

Opening the door without knocking, she found her beloved fiancé sitting calmly behind his desk. This time, she could see right through him ...

"What did you do to my professor?"

One Week Ago...

ENTERING THE LECTURE HALL, Lucca took an empty seat in the back, able to catch the ending of the professor's lecture. How lucky was he that Professor Miller taught a night class for working moms? And how lucky was he that Sal had been able to find that out on Professor Miller's Facebook page, where he couldn't help but post about it before each semester? The countless comments of women of all ages telling him what a "wonderful soul" he was to do such a thing brought a smile to his face, like Lucca was sure brought a smile to the professor's. What a kind and caring man Andy Miller was, and how grateful we should all be for his presence here at the university.

"Make sure you complete the questions 1, 5, and 6 in the review section at the end of the chapter. I expect the homework assignment to be completed by class tomorrow."

Lucca was sure that Chloe had gotten that exact assignment from his morning lecture.

Being only there for the last ten minutes, he wasn't sure how his fiancée could stay awake and listen to him for an hour so many times a week. He made his lectures about as interesting as watching paint dry. If it weren't for the professor's good looks, the room would be full of sleeping students. In fact, most of the male participants had to be awoken once the class was over.

He thought his life would be easier if Chloe pulled out of college, but there were some things Lucca knew he couldn't win. He only hoped his sanity would last a few more years until she graduated.

It wasn't until the last student had left that Lucca rose so the professor would notice him. There was someone else he needed to pay a visit to after this, and he would like to make it home before a new day began.

"Can I help you?" Professor Miller asked, packing up his things.

Lucca began stepping down the stairs of the pitched floor. "I believe so."

As he drew closer, the professor got a better view of him.

"I'm sorry, are you a student or future student?"

Lucca stopped before the final step. "Neither."

Professor Miller's eyes darted to the exit door at the top, the one he'd have to pass Lucca to get to. "Then I'm not sure how I can hel—"

"Chloe Masters."

Dawning realization had Miller's feet frozen to the floor. "Mr. Caruso, I'm not sure what you have been told, but Chloe and I—"

"You'd do well to address her as Ms. Masters, soon-to-be *Mrs.* Caruso." He let him know he shouldn't be on a first-name basis with his fiancée. "Not only in this conversation but in any capacity."

"S-sorry, you're correct." Professor Miller collected his nerves to start again. *"Ms. Masters and I* strictly have a student-teacher relationship."

"Well, I certainly hope not like the ..." Raising his hand, he began counting on his fingertips, saying a different name with each finger he lifted. "Oh, that's right, *eight* of the student-teacher relationships you've had in the past."

Professor Miller went about as gray as the hair that was peppered throughout his head.

"I mean to be completely honest. *I'm not one to talk,*" Lucca admitted his own gray area that the beginning of his and Chloe's relationship fell into. "Once might be forbidden true love ... but *eight* is a downright felony. You'd think by the seventh you might have learned your lesson, Professor Miller."

Swallowing hard, the professor knew he had been cornered. "Any relations I had were with *former* student—"

"Yeah, yeah, yeah." He waved him off, saving the spiel for the dean or court. "You're a real standup guy who waited till *after* they graduated."

"While maybe not the most ethical, I haven't done anything illegal, Mr. Caruso." Miller picked up his briefcase and went to leave, but the moment he got too close, he chickened out.

Lucca took the final step, closing any remaining

distance and letting the professor know just how close he wanted to get by getting on a first-name basis. "I'd suggest a change of scenery, Andy."

Nervous, *Andy* stammered, "I-it's the middle of the semester. W-where do you expect me to …?"

Lucca suddenly reached out, causing his words to drop off as he smoothed down the slightly wrinkled-up shoulders of his button-up shirt. He could practically feel the vibrations of the professor's bones rattling from the simple touch. Finally, he picked off the piece of lint that had driven him fucking crazy since he had spotted it ten minutes ago from all the way up the seats.

"Don't care where as long as the beautiful scenery isn't that of my fiancée." Hell, if Lucca was trying to go back to the old ways and be stared at as if he were in the *Godfather*, he might as well make the Italian leather shoe fit … "*Capiche?*"

I TOLD YOU I WOULDN'T
WHACK HIM

"Shut the door behind you, Chloe." Lucca used the same tone of voice he always used with her—gentle and soothing, as if pacifying a child.

The thought had any hesitations about confronting Lucca put aside. If they were going to get married, she had to make it plain and simple that she wasn't going to tolerate his interference in certain areas of her life.

She closed the door and came to stand in front of his desk. "I shut the door. Now answer my question."

Lucca raised a brow. "No kiss?"

She moved around the desk to kiss his waiting mouth, knowing what battles she could and would never win. Like when she went to move away yet found herself sitting on his lap. "Lucca …"

"Do you want an answer or not?"

This time, when she tried out Maria's death glare, it failed. She supposed Lucca was immune to it after growing up with the *originator* of the glare. Finally, Chloe quit struggling to get off his lap.

"I haven't done anything to Professor Miller."

"Then ... how did you know I was asking about Professor Miller?" Chloe knew she had him now, and worse, Lucca knew it, too.

"I *meant,* I didn't lay a hand on him." When Chloe tried the infamous glare on him again, he continued, "*Nor* did any of my men."

She crossed her arms over her chest. There was no fooling her this time.

"Then *what* exactly did you do?"

He thought for a moment, clearly weighing his words of how to best put it. "I *might* have strongly advised him to find another job."

At first, she wanted to

cry

scream

run ...

Hell, Chloe wasn't sure how she felt anymore, but what she did know was that none of that was going to work against a man they called the boogieman.

"Lucca, you *know* how much I love you. I mean, you *really* know. There was no need for you to break the trust I have in you just because you didn't want me around Professor Miller. Did you even consider another option? One where you were honest about your feelings?" Chloe guessed he hadn't from the brooding expression he was giving her. "You know you could have asked me to drop out of the class, right?"

"Why would I ask you to drop out of the class?" He picked up a lock of her shiny black hair to twine around his finger. "You weren't the person at fault."

"Neither was Professor Miller ..." Chloe's gray eyes drifted to the motion, too easily entranced. She drew her eyes back to his and stayed strong, like Maria had coached.

"He never spoke to me unless it was related to the class, Lucca. You took an argument I had *privately* with Adalyn and blew it out of proportion. Then you *mocked* that you wouldn't do anything to him." She had added the last part hoping it would drive her point home.

Unfortunately ... it did not.

He lightly tugged the strand of hair wrapped around his finger. "I wasn't mocking you. I told you I wouldn't *whack* him, and I didn't."

"No, he just won't be teaching at the college." She sighed when he still didn't get the point.

"There are other colleges and universities, darlin'. *Trust me*; I'm sure Professor Miller will *make do* with whatever place he decides to teach at next."

Not exactly sure what he was insinuating, her saddened gray eyes met his. "Lucca, don't you trust me?"

Letting go of the strand of hair, he used his finger to lift her porcelain chin. "Darlin', I trust *you*, just *not* men."

"It doesn't matter if you trust them if *you* trust *me*." Chloe's hand covered the one holding her chin. "If I felt Professor Miller was being inappropriate, I would have told you. I'm not a child whose judgment you can't trust."

With no response, Chloe thought back to Maria's last lesson ...

"NOW, when you still don't get what you want and everything else I've taught you fails"—Maria's emerald gaze grew serious—*"play dirty."*

LETTING GO OF HIM, she jumped off Lucca's lap. "My next class is tomorrow, and Professor Miller better be there."

His voice suddenly went dark. "He's not coming back."

WWMD. "Then I guess I'll move in with Elle and Nero until he does."

Lucca crossed his own arms, defiantly leaning back in his chair as he gave her his own glare. "Nero won't let you."

"I-I'll rent an apartment, then." Chloe was beginning to crack, but she hoped he wouldn't notice. "And I'll try to see you when I can."

"You're going to go there?" Lucca let her know he didn't like that, but then he softened. "Chloe, my main priority is your safety."

She bit her lip, and her eyes finally dropped to her feet. "You've left me with no choice, Lucca. I understand your need for my protection with the way your mother died." When Lucca started playing with his lighter, flipping it on and off, she stared into the flames. "But I'm not Melissa. Melissa was content to stay home behind guarded doors. I won't. I have dreams I want to fulfill. You're one of those dreams, but you're not my only one, any more than I can be the only one to fulfill what you want out of life."

Lucca held out his hand. "You're all I want, darlin'."

"You would be willing to walk away from being the head of the Caruso family? Let someone else take over?" Chloe took his hand. Sitting back down on his lap, she answered before he could, "I would never expect you to. That's what I'm trying to tell you. I don't want to become your whole world. You would get sick of just being with me."

He placed her hand on his chest so he could trace the scar on her lip. "No, I wouldn't."

"You would." She kissed him, knowing that was what he wanted. "But I love you somehow even more for saying that."

After giving him a few more kisses, she pulled her mouth away before it got too intense, knowing if they continued, she wouldn't be making it to her next class. "I need to get back to school."

Lucca groaned, regretfully letting her go.

"Now ..." Chloe smoothed down her outfit, trying to stand tall. "Will Professor Miller be back tomorrow, or should I start looking for an apartme—"

"He'll be back." He stopped her from speaking sacrilege. "*Now*, are you going to threaten to move out every time you get angry with me?"

"Only until we get married," Chloe joked with a smile as she moved toward the door.

His glare returned. "And what will you threaten me with then?"

Remembering the promise she had made her friend was the only reason she turned back, and definitely not how scary Lucca's voice had sounded to her. "Adalyn won't get in trouble for lending me her car?"

Lucca took his time answering, "No."

She knew he only conceded because he must've wanted her answer so badly. She was sure he wanted to be prepared for the future.

She thought for a moment but came up empty-handed. "I'll have to ask and get back to you later."

His eyes suddenly turned into slits. "Ask who?"

Sometimes, you just had to consult with the author ...

"Maria."

I SHOULD HAVE WHACKED HIM, Lucca thought when he entered the professor's home. Sure, it was unannounced and probably traumatic for him, but nothing warranted the goat-like, pussy-ass scream that came out of this grown man's mouth.

"I'm not going to kill you," he shouted over him, holding his hands up to the sky but not making any promises. "I'm just here to tell you that you better be at that podium, boring everyone to death, tomorrow morning."

The professor suddenly stopped screaming. "You want me to go back to work?"

"Unfortunately." Lucca was just as shocked that this was exactly what he was saying. "Now, is that going to be a problem?"

"No, no, of course not." Miller tried his best to appear appreciative. "I just didn't think you wanted me teaching Ch—I mean, Ms. Masters."

"Let's get one thing clear, Andy ... I don't." It took all of Lucca's strength not to have Chloe's professor showing up to class black and blue tomorrow. If he thought he could get away without her knowing it was him, he would be choking on his own words by now. "But you will show up tomorrow and teach my fiancée to the best of your abilities to ensure she will pass your class with flying colors."

When Miller nodded in understanding, Lucca continued as he took a threatening step closer.

"Now, if you stare even just a little bit too long in her direction, trust that I will find out about it. And, as for your record"—he let him know he hadn't forgotten about it—"it stays at *eight*."

The professor didn't need to hear the word *capiche* this time before he agreed. "Yes, of course."

Satisfied, Lucca almost turned to leave, forgetting something. When he reached inside his suit pocket, Miller went to scream again but stopped when he saw it was just a small piece of paper.

"What's this?" he asked, taking the slip that was held out to him.

"Names of my fiancée's friends who you also happen to teach. You'd do well to apply the same rules, as they're dating my men."

The professor's eyes grew wide at the first name, as it turned out Andy was one lucky motherfucker Lucca had found out about him first.

"If you think I'm jealous"—Lucca sinisterly smiled, wishing he hadn't—"then you don't want to meet my brother, Nero."

I'M SO SORRY, SWEETIE; WE'LL PRAY FOR YOU.

"There she is." Adalyn waved back at Gia before getting in line. "I thought by now she would have gotten tired of holding a table for us."

"Me, too," Chloe agreed, almost as surprised as she was earlier when she had seen Professor Miller standing behind the podium. "It's really nice of her."

Waiting to order, Elle nodded while her strawberry locks bounced. "I'll try to get here early tomorrow and pay for her lunch."

When they got their orders, they made their way to the large table Gia was holding for them.

"Hi." Instead of taking off today, she remained seated. "Do you mind if I sit and hang out for a while? My class just got canceled, so I have some time to blow."

Chloe unscrewed the top of her orange juice, grateful it was all she had gotten when she had seen Adalyn's nuggets were in the shape of different dinosaurs. "Your class got cancelled?"

"Just got the email," Gia confirmed, seemingly not irritated about it in the slightest. "Well, at least I was able to save you guys from having to eat at the picnic tables outside. It's supposed to rain."

"We really appreciate you." Elle smiled at her sweetly, speaking for all of them. "I don't know how you always manage to get here early every day."

"Me, either." Adalyn grimaced. "I'd show up later if I could, but Chloe is always a pain in the ass if we're even just a millisecond late."

Chloe practically spit out her OJ. "I am not."

"You are, too." Adalyn looked over at Elle for backup.

Her best friend pled the fifth.

Okay, maybe they're a little right but ... "I just don't understand how one person would need to set ten alarms to make it to school on time."

"Well, you'd think I was a freaking saint if you had to be at school as the same time as Lake." Adalyn dunked a chicken nugget into the BBQ sauce. "Speaking of ..."

"Sorry I'm late." Lake slid into the spot next to Adalyn. "What did I miss? Anything good?"

"Nope. We just sat down." Elle clearly hoped they didn't have to have the last conversation all over again. However, the tall brunette felt like she had missed out on something juicy.

"Oh, I thought something was going on with Gia still here."

Adalyn quickly filled her in, speaking so fast that none of them knew how Lake was even able to keep up.

"Yeah, my first class starts after lunch," Lake said, picking up her apple. "I get here early to eat with the girls, but Vincent always makes me late by hitting snooze on my phone. He works late nights," she added, making excuses on her boyfriend's behalf. "If anyone should be here early to get us a table, it should be me, so I'm sorry for that."

"No worries." Gia shrugged. "Honestly, my roommate is a music major, so having a reason to leave my dorm room early saves me from having to buy her a new instrument because I broke it."

"Oh no," all the girls said in unison, with varying tones as if someone had just died.

Chloe gulped loudly, while Elle was the only one brave enough to ask, "What does she play?"

"*Clarinet.*"

Each one gave her their own pitying look around the table.

Adalyn leaned forward to pat her hand, able to find the words on behalf of all of them. "I'm so sorry, sweetie; we'll pray for you."

"M-maybe you should ask for another roommate?" Chloe offered, knowing God had more important matters to attend to than a clarinet.

"I have," Gia huffed. "There aren't any available."

"Stay with some friends," Adalyn urged, dunking another nugget in sauce.

Their new lunch buddy's face fell. "I would, but I actually haven't made any here. This is my first semester. I'm from Tennessee."

"That's strange," Lake said, swallowing a bite of her apple. "You don't have an accent."

"Speech therapy. Lisp," Gia explained quickly before continuing on. "I worked two years to save my money so I could afford to come here."

They listened as they ate their food. Chloe was just as interested as the rest of them.

"Why here?"

"My major is husbandry."

Adalyn's jaw dropped just as she was about to pop

another nugget into her mouth. "You can major in how to get a husband?"

At first, Chloe wanted to laugh, but then she realized *she* didn't know what the hell husbandry was.

"Husbandry is the study of crops and cattle," Lake explained—she had family from Kentucky. "I just don't know why you'd come to Missouri to study it when Tennes—"

"So, what's your major?" Gia asked Adalyn.

"I'm winging it." She shrugged, finally able to eat her nugget now that her jaw wasn't on the floor. "Whatever *Chloe* is majoring in, *I'm* majoring in. She's my ticket to graduating."

Gia stared at Adalyn as if she didn't know how to respond to that, so she looked toward Chloe. "What are you and Adalyn majoring in?"

"Pre-law," Chloe answered.

"We are?" Adalyn's mouth dropped back to the floor.

"You are?" Elle asked, searching her eyes to see if she was telling the truth.

"Since when?" Adalyn continued, still stunned.

Chloe fiddled with the cap of her OJ then finally confided in her friends, "I-I've been thinking of it for a while." She was mumbling under her breath, but at least Lake understood why she'd want to be.

"That'll come in handy."

"How are you going to be a lawyer? You're the most non-confrontational person I know."

Chloe didn't take any offense to Adalyn's questioning, knowing it was an honest one and what she said was, in fact, true.

"I'm winging it."

Elle glared at Adalyn then turned to give her best friend an encouraging smile. "I believe in you."

Smiling back, she knew one thing to be true—*you always have*—but Chloe couldn't miss that Adalyn was upset.

"What's wrong?"

"Becoming a lawyer takes too long!" she cried, practically in tears.

Lake tried to get her BFF to cheer up. "You can just stay undecided with me, and we'll take a bunch of different classes together again."

Adalyn stared at her balefully, knowing she'd never graduate that way. The best thing that had happened to her grades was Chloe leaving Stanford to come to the university here with them.

"You could take English classes with me ..." Elle offered.

Somehow, Adalyn managed to look even *more* upset. "Did you forget I had to take *remedial* English."

"Oh." Elle gave her a sympathetic glance. "Sorry. I forgot."

Left with no other option, Adalyn turned her gaze back to Gia. "What's your GPA?"

"*Adalyn!*" Lake's elbow came out to hit her for being nosy.

"Uh ..." Gia awkwardly laughed. "I have a 3.9."

"Not bad." Adalyn smiled brightly. "We should get to know each other better, maybe take some classes togeth—"

"What are you going to do with crops and cattle?" Lake hissed at her.

An unsure Gia started gathering her backpack and tray.

Not wanting to lose them their future lunch tables, Chloe stepped in. "S-she gets carried away sometimes."

Elle rushed to speak before Gia could leave, too, knowing what her best friend was thinking. "Let's exchange numbers. We go shopping or have movie nights with our other friends a couple of times a month. You're welcome to come. I can text you the next time we all hang out together if you wanted to join?"

"Yeah, you should totally come hang out with us!" Lake agreed before she none-to-sneakily hit her bestie under the table, knowing the responsibility would fall on her to get her ass here early to grab a lunch table if Adalyn managed to fuck this up.

You could tell the lightbulb hadn't gone off in her head that she was beginning to freak Gia out, but Adalyn smiled and nodded in agreement, at least able to figure out that was what Lake wanted her to do.

"I guess ... it would be nice to have friends to hang out with off campus," Gia finally agreed, giving them her number before she left. When she did, she gave Adalyn's side of the table a wide berth.

"Did I miss something?" Adalyn asked in a hushed voice as she looked at them. "Why was she acting so weird?"

Lake loved Adalyn too much to tell her the truth. "She probably had to go to the bathroom."

Chloe and Elle stared at each other, neither of them wanting to hurt her feelings, either.

"You want to be a lawyer, Chloe? Prove it," Adalyn dared her. "You can't be afraid to hurt people's feelings."

"Um ..." Chloe looked into her friend's eyes, preparing to tell her the unadulterated truth. "Adalyn, sometimes ..."

Rolling her eyes, Adalyn bit the head off her dino nugget. "Oh, just spit it out already!"

Welp, someone has to say it.

"College isn't for everyone."

A PROMISE ONLY A BOOGIEMAN
COULD KEEP

It was already Friday as Chloe walked up to the Caruso family home. Lately, she and Lucca spent the weekdays at the Casino Hotel, while they spent their weekends here.

Waving goodbye to Henry, she opened the front door to find flickering tea lights winding a path upstairs. Warmth began to fill her heart at knowing he was trying to make up for their fight earlier in the week. He had even already set the table romantically with long, tapering candles and flowers.

Damn, she was going to have to thank Maria the next time she saw her; she was a freaking miracle worker.

Entering their bedroom, she found it empty as the tea lights continued to the bathroom. She dropped her backpack onto a chair before she walked inside to see Lucca waiting for her in the steaming tub.

Amused, she sat on the edge of the bath. "Is this an apology?"

"No. This is me making amends."

Chloe raised a scarred brow. "There's a difference?"

"I don't have to say I'm sorry *if* I'm making amends," he stated simply.

Knowing her fiancé didn't have the word *sorry* in his vocabulary, she continued to tease him, wanting to milk this whole "non" apology for all she could. "You don't?"

Waving the water, he hoped to entice her. "At least not until you get in."

Chloe didn't have to be told twice. She quickly took off her clothes, carefully stepped over the edge to immerse herself in the warmth, then laid her head back on the awaiting cushioned bath pillow.

A hungry-eyed Lucca spread his legs to allow her more room as he took one of her feet in his hands to massage it.

No, Maria was no miracle worker; she was *the man whisperer*.

"I could get used to this." Chloe sighed, her toes curling in pleasure. "I should get angry at you more often if this what I have to look forward to."

"I'm just setting the bar high for you for when I get angry at you." Switching feet, Lucca skillfully started kneading her other foot.

"I'm never going to do anything to make you mad at me." And both of them knew that to be true.

Yawning, she had to grab the side of the tub when Lucca used her foot to pull her closer to him, forcing her legs to wrap around him.

"You can't go to sleep yet, darlin'." His lips went to her jaw, placing tender kisses along it. "I made us a special dinner, then we're going to make passionate love while I tell you I'm sorry. I have it all planned out."

"You never do anything halfway," she murmured appreciatively as he now trailed kisses over her collarbone.

"Not when it comes to you," he admitted wholeheartedly.

All sleepiness gone, Chloe gazed at the man she was about to pledge her life to, amazed that he still wanted her when he could have his choice of any woman in Kansas City.

Sliding her bottom on the tub, she pressed her breasts to his chest. "Dante and Melissa must have loved each other very much." Her words came out in a whisper.

Lucca gazed back at her quizzically. "You sound pretty sure considering you never saw them together."

"I didn't have to. They created four beautiful children, and you"—Chloe smiled sweetly—"were their masterpiece."

"I'll never deserve your love." His voice turned a bit gruff while his eyes fiercely bore into her gray depths. "I wish I could be the man I see in your eyes, but I'll never be. There won't be a place for me in heaven, and I can't let you go there one day thinking I'll be there waiting for you, Chloe."

The thought of a life without Lucca was incomprehensible to her, and she was sure it was the same for him.

"There's no way of knowing which one of us is going to die first."

Lucca's blue-green eyes no longer pierced hers, but her soul. "Darlin', not even God is powerful enough to take you away from me as long as there's breath in my body."

"Careful, Lucca, I wouldn't tempt Him to prove you wron—"

He laughed. Like everything else, Lucca wasn't afraid of any man, and especially not the big guy upstairs. "I'll to go confession if you want, but it's still the truth."

Elle had once warned her that, when Lucca got angry, everyone in Kansas City locked their doors, but God help her, when Lucca was good ... *he was* so *good.* He made her heart melt, and any concerns about what he was capable of melted away with it. Lucca was more religious than she was, and if the pearly gates weren't going to open for Lucca, she didn't much care if they didn't open for her, either.

"You don't have to. I don't want to go to heaven if you won't be there."

"Doesn't matter if God keeps me out. Besides"—he made it clear there was no need to feel sorry for him—"my heaven is right here, with you."

Letting him take her mouth in a hard kiss, she slid her wet arms around his shoulders to hold him tighter. Lucca was right; what they shared together *was* heaven on Earth.

Cupping her bottom, he lifted her up to slide her down onto his cock.

Careful not to get carried away so the water wouldn't spill over, she lightly rocked over him. Lucca, however, wasn't as restrained, thrusting his hips. She had to hold on tight to the sides to stay inside the tub.

She would have tried to calm him, but it felt too good. Letting go of her reserve, she held on tighter, trying to match his movements as she sought to give Lucca the same ecstasy he was giving her.

As they climaxed together, they held each other tightly, their bodies shaking as the water cooled around them.

Not before she was done shaking did Lucca lift himself and her out of the tub to wrap her up in a warm towel. They dressed before going downstairs, hand in hand, to eat the dinner he had prepared for them.

They were eating dessert when Lucca's face went stern.

"Promise me that you won't run off from your security like that again. The next time you want to let me have it and

I'm not within shouting distance, call me, and I'll come to you."

The commanding way he was talking to her had her newfound independence wanting to argue back. It wasn't until she looked into his eyes that she saw the true fear there.

"I'll never do it again," she promised. "I'll wait until I get home."

Happy with her response, Lucca rose and blew out the candles before he picked her right up from her chair. "Be sure to call me on the way to give me a heads-up. That way, I can have the bath ready."

She wrapped her arms tightly around his neck. "I won't plan on it working every time."

Laying her head on his shoulder as he brought her up the stairs, she was so content. Nothing, absolutely nothing, could mar the happiness she felt.

In their bedroom, Lucca disrobed her then took off his own clothes before laying her down on the bed. "I would have you painted in this position, but I would have to kill the painter when he was finished."

Taking it at a joke, Chloe laughed. "Elle and Adalyn compared you to Ted Bundy and Skeet Ulrich in *Scream*."

A searing kiss on the inside of her upper thigh had her stomach quivering at the intimate touch.

"What did you say to them?"

Another searing kiss landed in the top curve of her thigh as his mouth moved higher. Chloe was so entranced in what he was doing she wouldn't have been able to spell her last name if he had asked.

"I can't remember," she panted.

"Darlin', I wouldn't harm a spider." Lucca's tongue swept over her clit then swept back, as if he was tasting ice cream for the first time. "I mean, they could have at least compared me to a better group of men."

"You mean men who *aren't* serial killers?" she asked as she wiggled herself lower to get the best benefit of his torturing tongue.

"No." Removing his tongue to replace it with a long, teasing finger, Lucca glanced up at her fleetingly. "Amateurs."

She gasped when his finger parted her wider so Lucca could glide his dick expertly inside her.

Unsure what he meant by them being amateurs, she lost all thought when he took her wrists and pinned them over her head. She swore he could make her feel each hard thrust in every cell of her body, holding her eyes just as easily as he controlled her body.

Through heavy-lidded eyes, Chloe managed to catch a brief glimpse of the real Lucca with his guard down. His visage in this brief moment was different than the comfortable, reassuring man she was used to seeing. Tonight, Chloe caught sight of the ruthless, arrogant, dark man whom her friends had warned her about. They hadn't been teasing; they had been trying to warn her. She now understood his comment—Lucca considered them to be amateurs because ...

They got caught.

Then, suddenly, in the blink of an eye, *her* Lucca was back.

"Is something wrong?" Loosening his grip on her wrists, he linked his fingers with hers.

She gripped his fingers back, trying to desperately hang on. "No, nothing."

The scared Chloe who was always afraid of her own shadow wanted to run away, but the *new* Chloe was braver, willing to accept she loved Lucca enough to love *both* sides of him ...

Her lover.

And the boogieman.

Her revelation sent her climax spiraling out of control.

"Lucca ..." she screamed out, unable to hold it inside.

As she fell back to earth from the orgasmic bliss he had carried her to, she returned to awareness with his arms surrounding her protectively.

"You caught me," she mumbled, exhaustion overtaking her.

"I always will, darlin'."

Chloe heard the reassuring promise follow her into the depths of her sleep. It was a promise only a boogieman could keep.

A SUSPECT

As he was gardening with Chloe, it wasn't until every hair on his body stood on end that his instincts told him someone was near.

Looking through the glass windows, he was able to see the man inside his family home not only *uninvited*, but *unannounced*. Fear chilled his bones, knowing it could have almost been too late.

"Stay here," he instructed her.

"Okay." Chloe could tell he was upset about something, so she didn't dare to argue.

Wiping the dirt off his hands and onto his jeans, he slipped through the back door. Carefully, he watched the back of the man in a tailored suit and brimmed hat he recognized, but only just for a moment before he decided to let his presence be known.

"Enzo."

Enzo spun on the heel of his Italian leather shoes. "Hello, Lucca."

"Sorry." Amo came barreling in to finally join them in the room. "I—"

Holding up a hand, Lucca silenced him. There were only a few men left he trusted these days, and almost all of them had women of their own to protect from One-Shot. While the relationship he had with his soldier was complicated, he did at least trust him enough to protect Chloe.

Or so I thought.

"Go outside and watch over Chloe." His commanding tone held a threat that he better not fuck that up either.

Nodding, Amo's head slightly hung as he went out the back door ...

CHLOE WIPED the bead of sweat that kissed her brow, hoping everything was all right.

When the back door opened and Amo appeared, she realized he must've been instructed to come watch over her as he put his back to the door and crossed his arms. Her security had been instructed to be invisible to her lately, so to say she was shocked to find out Lucca had chosen him as their security detail for the weekend was a *massive* understatement.

She nervously picked the shovel back up. It was the first time her and Amo had been alone since they'd spoke at the Casino Hotel the last time. Their conversation hadn't gone like she had hoped and, regretfully, in choosing Lucca, she had lost a friend in the process.

She bit her lip as her eyes drifted between him and the ground while she fiddled with the dirt. No longer did she know the Amo before her. That Amo had died upon her breaking his heart, but she'd swear she could see the disappointment in his eyes no matter how much he was trying to hide it.

With her eyes drifting back to the ground, she pulled up the roots of the dead flower only to reveal the new bud that had been burgeoning beneath.

Looking back up, Chloe smiled peacefully at an old friend. "Hi, Amo."

"Don't blame him for my intrusion," Enzo said sympathetically as the door clicked shut. "As his father, I'm able to hide my presence from my son."

"You're lucky to be alive," Lucca warned him what the cost of dodging his son could have been. "If I didn't know the back of you so well, *and that ugly hat*, you'd be dead."

"I'd have more than one soldier guarding the home," Enzo gave some fatherly advice while his eyes slid to look out to the backyard to the view. "Especially with *her* here."

Lucca's jaw flexed as he turned to see his fiancée's pale skin almost sparkling in the sunlight, sitting there as beautiful as a rose, and just as *ripe* for the taking.

It wasn't that Enzo was necessarily wrong, because he did have a point, but his Capo just didn't take into account that they'd have to get through him to get to Chloe, *and hell help the man who tried.*

He stepped to the side to block Enzo's view of his fiancée. Then his words came out in a frustrated hiss. "Why are you here, Enzo?"

"I've requested to speak with you, but"—bending his neck, he took his hat off—"I've been turned down every time."

"Because I've been busy," Lucca reminded him.

Enzo's eyes trailed down to his dirt-stained dark jeans. "Yes, I see."

122

If Enzo De Santis weren't one of his father's best friends, he would have fucking killed him where he stood, because at the moment, it definitely wasn't his son, Amo, nor his brother, Drago, who was keeping him breathing.

"As your boss"—taking a threatening step toward him, Lucca knew exactly why he was here—"I'm considering my options for who I want to sit underneath me."

"Ah." Enzo looked down with the same sad expression Amo had a moment ago. Spinning the hat around in his hands, he forced a smile. "I suppose we *all* get *old* someday."

"It's not about age, Enzo." He didn't know how to put in words his reasoning of why he hadn't just given him his old placeholder position back ... until he did. "It's about trust."

"Right. *Well* ..." A fully understanding Enzo bent his head to set the hat back in its place. "I suppose I'll be going, then."

"I think that's best," Lucca agreed.

As a family friend, he had seen the tall, slender man leave a thousand times over the years, but lately, he hadn't looked at him that way but as a Capo.

Now, however, Lucca looked at Enzo De Santis in a whole new light.

Not as a Caporegime, but ...

*As a suspec*t.

SURPRISE, MOTHERFUCKER

Chloe woke at Lucca's kiss.

"I brought you breakfast."

Becoming wide awake, she sat up so Lucca could set the tray down over her lap. There was no way this was part of the apology.

"What did I do deserve this?"

"Just want your day started off right." Lucca shrugged like it was no big deal. "I want you wide awake so the girls won't be able to convince you of some hideous color for their bridesmaids' dresses." Suddenly, his mood soured. "If Vincent tells me one more time yellow isn't his fucking color, I'm going to *whack* him."

Chloe giggled. "You wouldn't."

Lucca's face showed no trace of humor.

"Okay, no yellow. Got it. Any other colors I should stay away from?" she asked, making a mental note, but even she didn't expect the boogieman's answer.

"Black," Lucca instructed, not wanting to see her in that color on their wedding day. "Black is for funerals. Our wedding is to be a celebration."

Considering her wardrobe consisted of only black clothing, she was growing nervous of the thought of her in a wedding gown. "All right, no black."

Frowning, Lucca brushed the veil of hair that was covering her scar behind her ears. "I thought you would be more excited about planning our wedding?"

"I-I am."

He picked up the butter knife and smeared butter across a piece of toast. "I don't believe you."

Chloe took the toast away from him. "I can understand why you want a big wedding, I really do. It's just ... I don't like being the center of attention. What if I trip as I walk down the aisle? All I really wanted was a small wedding with us, Elle, and Nero, in a secluded spot. Then we could just go to a nice restaurant where you and Nero could argue about who cooks the steaks better—you or the chef."

"We could do that, if you prefer."

Lucca's sincere expression had her about to wrap her arms around his neck in happiness. Then guilty thoughts about who would be left out intruded, and she didn't want them to feel bad they hadn't been invited.

"Maria could come ..." she hastily inserted.

"Dom wouldn't want her coming alone."

"Okay, then he can come, too," she agreed.

"I wouldn't hear the end of it from Vincent if a Luciano was there and he and Amo weren't."

"They can come." Chloe wouldn't want them to feel left out. "Lake and Adalyn, too ..."

Lucca raised a brow. "No Kat and Angel?"

Quickly, the simple wedding plans went right down the drain. "We can do the big wedding. It's just my nerves getting to me."

Smiling, he made her an oath, "I promise you won't trip, darlin', and I'll be there to catch you if you do."

"Okay ..." She smiled back sweetly. "Oh, and if you can promise One-Shot won't *whack* one our guests, I just *might* dance."

Lucca's eyes narrowed. "You're never going to let me get away from saying *whack*, are you?"

"No." Her laughter spilled out at his pained expression.

Buttering another spear of toast, he ate it in one bite before getting off the bed. "Now, hurry up. Your friends are waiting for you. The shop has called *twice* already to confirm the appointment, so you don't want to be late. I also have a special surprise when you're done with the fittings."

A surprise? Setting the tray aside, Chloe jumped out of bed, knowing when it came to surprises, her fiancé never went halfway. "What is it?"

"You'll have to wait and see, darlin' ..." he teased. "And because I'm such *good* fiancé, I even let Adalyn invite your new friend."

"Gia?"

Lucca nodded.

Yikes. She mumbled what she thought was indiscernible under her breath, "You should have let Elle or Lake invite her."

"Why not Adal—"

"No reason." Rising up on her tiptoes, she placed a tender kiss on his lips. "You told me not to be late!"

Leaving her confused fiancé, she went to get dressed for the day and was ready and downstairs in what seemed like no time to find a serious Lucca on the phone in the kitchen. While she had been trying to pick an outfit to wear, he must've gotten dressed, as he was freshly showered and donned in his all-black tailored suit.

He ended the call and tucked his phone into his suit pocket, and when he spoke, his face was about as serious as his expression had been. "Vincent and Amo will be your security today. I expect you to remain in their eyesight at all times."

It wasn't instructions from her fiancé, but from the boss.

"Understand?" he asked, raising her chin with a finger when she didn't respond.

Chloe could only manage a nod. Her breath was stuck in her throat by how dark the beautiful man before her was.

He leaned down to give her a parting kiss. It was the first time she had kissed the boogieman when he was dressed to kill...

AFTER SAYING his goodbyes to Chloe, Lucca rushed to the Casino Hotel after getting a phone call about an emergency in the underground casino. When he made it to the hidden bottom floor, he went down the dark hallway and through the door that was supposed to have been guarded by one of his soldiers.

It was pitch black when he first went in, but then the lights suddenly flicked on and ...

"*Surprise!*" everyone yelled as the place lit up.

Speechless, Lucca looked around to see all his and Dominic's men had come to congratulate him on his promotion. He probably heard "Congrats, boss" a thousand times as he went through the sea of suits that was gambling, drinking, and beginning to have a good time.

Coming up to an ear-to-ear smiling Sal, he knew exactly who had been responsible.

"Like it?" Sal asked, proud of himself.

Lucca looked down at the cake that had the words "Surprise, Motherfucker" written in icing.

"You *really* shouldn't have."

THE TAPPING of heels as Chloe was being scrutinized had her wishing a sink hole would appear in the ground and swallow her whole.

She hadn't liked any of the dresses the girls had picked out to even come out of the dressing room yet, and neither had Maria or the sales associate, Ken, who beat at his red-bottom shoes, trying to decide what to put her in next.

"You know what ...?" A lightbulb turned on in Ken's head, his voice trailing off as he dashed away. He was back in mere moments with a dress in hand. "This came in just this morning. It hasn't been pressed yet, which is why it wasn't on the floor."

Chloe took one look at the simple yet elegant dress and fell in love. While her flamboyant sister-in-law didn't yet seem convinced, she still left the room to let her get changed, returning to her place in the waiting area on the couch.

Chloe walked out of the room, stepped up onto the pedestal, and nervously smoothed the white dress down over her wide hips. With it being so simple, it put her curvy figure on display, and the square neckline, while still modest, complemented her large breasts.

Her girlfriends still, in complete silence, Chloe somehow grew even more nervous when she had to ask, "Well, what do you think?"

Elle, her forever BFF, spoke for them all, "I *love* it."

However, Maria must still not have been convinced when she asked Ken to get something else from the back.

Ken left again, this time not returning with a dress but a big box.

A pregnant Maria stood and opened the lid. Then she magically pulled out a beautiful white veil that seemed like it went on for miles.

Every girl's mouth fell open in a gasp, including Chloe's.

"I had this made for you," Maria said, approaching her to place the beautiful veil on her head as tears began to fall from the all the girls' eyes.

"Oh, Maria." Chloe was in awe looking at what seemed like a million roses that trailed down it with tears brimming her own eyes. "It's *beautiful*."

Maria started sniffling. Pulling a tissue from the box Ken held out, she dared anyone to say anything, like the pregnancy was the reason for making her so emotional. When she finally looked at Chloe, she didn't look at her like she was to be her future sister-in-law; Maria looked at her as if she were a sister ...

"Mom would have loved it."

"WHAT ARE WE DOING HERE, LUCCA?" Dominic asked under his breath when he came to stand beside him.

Lucca's eyes drifted across the room, scrutinizing each person at the party. "You know *exactly* what."

"We've been here for over two hours."

Raising his wrist, he checked his watch to see the Luciano mob boss was right; they had been here for over two hours already. The "surprise" party was about as fake as the tits of the women who worked down here, but only a few he trusted knew.

"If he was going to show, he would have done it already," Dom stated, sure to keep his voice low.

"Oh, he'll show." Lucca didn't doubt that for a second. Like Dom's wife, his sister had said, One-Shot was into the theatrics.

He could never *miss a good party.*

"You sure that's a good thing?" An antsy Dominic looked around the room to see practically every made man in the city was gathered here. "We're fucking sitting ducks."

PRO TIP: GIVE ADALYN SKITTLES TO MAKE HER SHUT UP

Once the fittings were over, they went out to the stretch limo Lucca had gifted them for the day. Adalyn jumped up and down on the luxurious upholstery. "What are we doing next?"

"I don't know." Chloe was just as excited and clueless as the others. "Lucca said it's a special surprise. I guess we'll find out when we get there."

"You want me to ask Vincent?" Lake asked, moving to where she could knock on the barrier separating the front of the car from the back. "He might tell me."

Elle stopped her. "No, let's not spoil Lucca's surprise."

"Ooo ... You think he's going to splurge and give us a shopping trip?" Lake's eyes grew wide at the thought, though Maria quickly burst her balloon.

"Knowing *my* brother, that would be a *no*."

Amo didn't park the limo in the parking lot. Instead, he went behind the mall to park next to a back door to one of the businesses.

Amo opened the door for them. "This is it."

They all piled out excitedly. Chloe let her guests go first, getting out last.

"What about Gia? I invited her—"

"She's already inside. Lucca had an Uber sent for her."

Relieved Gia hadn't been forgotten, she went up the stone steps to the back door marked *"Private Entrance Staff Only."*

Using a key, a quieter-than-usual Vincent unlocked the door. It was obvious Lucca had read him his rights and had told him that he better be on his best behavior today.

Following him inside, they went up two flights of stairs, coming to a metal door that a man in a dark suit was holding open for them.

Walking in last, with Amo right behind her, she heard her friends' excited yells before she could see anything, and when she finally did, Chloe saw why they were all yelling and why her best friend's yell had been the loudest.

They were standing smack-dab in an empty movie theater. The front entrance was closed; no one allowed inside except for them and the staff. The *"Now Showing"* posters had all been replaced with some of their favorite movies—*Bridesmaids, Fifty First Dates, Titanic, Scream, The Little Mermaid, A Walk to Remember, The Notebook, Pride and Prejudice, Dirty Dancing,* and *Twilight.*

An awestruck Elle stared at the posters. "I have died and gone to heaven."

"Oh God, Nero and I are fucked. We ain't never gonna hear the end of this." Whatever spell Vincent was under had started to fade with each scrutinizing glance Lake was giving him. "How the hell am I supposed to top thi—"

Amo elbowed him, clearly to remind him of something.

Chloe was still taking it all in. She looked at Maria as

her eyes started to brim with tears for the second time today. "Did you bring any tissues with you?"

"No, but *I wish* I had." Maria looked like she wanted to cry, too, but not with happiness.

Kat gave her a *kill me, please* look, letting Maria know she felt her pain when she saw a big cutout of Edward Cullen.

The manager stepped forward to introduce himself.

"Ms. Masters, your fiancé has rented the theater for the rest of the day and night. The staff will provide you with anything you want. As you see, we have hamburgers, hotdogs, nachos, popcorn. All you have to do is order, and we will have it prepared to your liking. You may choose from any of the movies on the wall. As you get your food and snacks, I'll let the projectionist know which movie you have chosen first. What shall it be?"

Too excited to choose, she looked at her friends. "What should we watch first, guys?"

Ordering a tub of popcorn with triple butter, Elle gave her suggestion. "We should watch *Titanic* first. It's the longest."

Knowing her best friend was thinking tactfully, she began the movie list order in her head.

"Gia?" She let her choose next, wanting her to feel more comfortable.

Poor Gia looked as if she had been catapulted into another dimension, clearly not knowing what she had signed up for. Her eyes moved down the line at the different movies. "No *Fifty Shades of Grey*?"

Maria gave her an approving smile. "I think I'm going to like you, whoever you are."

Chloe quickly introduced her to Maria and Kat. "Sorry,

Gia. Lucca told me he had a surprise for me. I just didn't expect all this."

Gia stared at her. "Your fiancé did this?"

Chloe nodded, becoming teary again.

"Does he have a brother?"

"Yes, two. Nero, who's Elle's boyfriend, and Leo is his younger brother. Maria's their sister," she said, making more introductions to help Gia understand better.

Gia, however, was still caught on catching a brother. "How much younger?"

Chloe laughed. "He's still in high school."

Disappointed, Gia looked through the movie posters again. "*Scream*."

"Now we're talking," a pink-haired Kat yelled out while filling her hands with candy. "Any chance we could watch *Scream* twice?"

Chloe shook her head doubtfully, knowing they were going to be lucky to get through half of them. "Maria?" she asked for her choice, moving on.

At this point, the beautiful blonde only had one request. "Anything but *Pride and Prejudice*."

Chloe made a mental note to put that one in dead last, because even though she was happily married, she knew the last thing Maria wanted to watch was sisters trying to find a man all because they needed to wed to secure their futures.

"Then we can watch *The Little Mermaid*," Chloe added to the list, wanting to make sure they had time to watch Elle and her favorite movie.

Lake's sights, however, weren't set on a Disney film. "I choose *Dirty Dancing* next, then."

Vincent couldn't help but roll his eyes as he mumbled under his breath, "What's so special about Patrick Swayze?"

Kat threw a gummy worm at him as if she had a

Luciano vendetta against him. "Well, for starters, he can dance."

"I can—ow!" Vincent rubbed his shoulder where Amo had struck him but decided to keep his pretty mouth shut.

His sister, Adalyn, who had been awfully quiet as she loaded up two hotdogs and a barrel of soda, clearly gave zero fucks what was going to play on the screen. "All right, let's get the party started. Lake, can you get the family-size of peanut M&M's?" she asked, placing a bag of Skittles between her teeth. They were just barely able to make out the rest as she mumbled, "My hands are full."

Chloe made another mental note while she was at it.

Pro tip: Give Adalyn Skittles to make her shut up.

"DOMINIC LUCIANO," Vinny Vitale greeted him regally as he joined them in the corner. "How have you been?"

"Never better." He held out his left tatted hand.

Vinny reached out to shake it. Unable to miss the jewelry on his ring finger, he smiled. "I'm glad the arrangement I struck has worked out for all of us."

"Yeah," he huffed. "*Finally.*"

Lucca gave the man who had managed to land the throne and his sister all in the same year a patronizing look. *Yeah, poor you.*

"I've been thinking about what you asked, Lucca." The consigliere turned to him. "And I think I came up with a solution."

"That so?"

The consigliere waved his hand as he spoke, "Yes. How about I stop by your office tomorrow so we can discuss the matter?"

His eyes went back to scrutinizing the men. He would find out tomorrow how to best handle his men when they found out he was to wed a woman without Italian descent. "Sounds good."

"Great." Turning to leave, Vinny turned back for just a moment. "Oh, and do you happen to know where my son is?"

It might not be the truth, as he knew exactly where his soldier ought to be, but it was still pretty much accurate.

"With Vincent ... God only knows."

DO YOU KNOW WHO HE IS?

P ressing *Send* on the black heart emoji, she sent it to Lucca's phone. She knew he would understand that it meant she was not only grateful but also thinking about him.

When she returned her eyes to the big screen, she realized she probably shouldn't have drunk all that soda. She began to squirm in her seat. All the water in the scene where the Titanic was about to go down and everyone was clinging for life wasn't helping. She didn't want to miss the best part ...

Gia's whisper revealed her own predicament. "I need to go, too."

It made her feel better to know Gia was in the same boat. "If we hurry, we can be back before Leo dies."

With Gia beating her to get up, Chloe didn't need any other encouragement.

Vincent was the only one who paid them any attention when they stood. He had been guarding the theater by stationing himself at the exit door next to the movie screen, while Amo had taken position at the back of the theater, where he could guard the other door. All the other girls had been too engrossed in the movie, even Maria and Kat, who would swear later they weren't. None of them clearly wanted to chance missing the part coming up as they slid their legs out of the way, so Gia and Chloe could get through. Chloe didn't blame them; the part where Rose swears she'll never let go ... only to *let him* fucking *go* ... was iconic.

"We need a bathroom break," she explained when Amo stepped outside the doors with them.

Nodding, he walked them to the restroom and stood about five steps away in front of the men's bathroom.

Hurrying to do their business, the two relieved girls met up at the wash station.

"Phew, I had been holding it in since Rose was trying to get the damn key in the lock." The relief looked real on Gia's face in the mirror. "I thought Adalyn would be the first to go with how much soda she drank."

Chloe couldn't help but laugh. "Adalyn has a bladder of steel. She'll probably make it until the end of the next movie."

The threw their paper towels away and walked out of the restroom in a hurry to get back.

Focused solely on what part of the movie she was missing, she automatically took a step toward the theater door. At the same time, it finally registered in her brain that Amo wasn't standing where they had left him. Then her arm was grabbed.

Startled at the sudden touch, her eyes flew to the side, completely dismayed at who was holding her arm, but she didn't immediately pull away. "What are—"

"Lucca sent me after you. We need to go. There's been an emergency."

Gia was just as startled as she was. Grabbing Chloe's other arm, she held her firmly in place at the urgent demand. "Do you know who he is?"

She could barely think as her heart pounded out of her chest. "Y-yes, he's ..."

Lucca headed to talk with Sal when ...

"Lucca."

Turning at his name, Lucca saw an apologetic Enzo taking off his hat.

"I wanted to apologize for yesterday. I shouldn't have shown up like that." Nervously spinning the hat, he appeared sincere. "I should have respected you and your fiancée's privacy. It won't happen again."

Lucca nodded his head warily with slight suspicion, giving him a direct warning. "I hope *not*."

"It won't." An anxious laugh escaped Enzo's throat before he cleared it. "I hope I didn't frighten your fiancée by showing up unannounced like that."

Lucca's jaw tightened.

"Where ... *is* she, by the way?" he asked, glancing around the room. "I don't see any of the girls here celebrating, actually."

"Girls' night," he said through gritted teeth before he forced himself to relax. It took all of Lucca's strength to keep up the charade. Each of them who knew the plan was to spread the same lie about the girls' whereabouts in hopes to snare their trap. "Having a movie night in Nero's penthouse."

"Well, I hope they have a wonderful time." Placing his

hat back on his head, he gave him a goodbye wave with it before he did. "Great party."

As he watched the back of what he believed now to be One-Shot walk away, he didn't let him out of his sight as Sal approached him, coming to see him instead.

"Everything all right?"

"For now. Just don't let anyone out of your sight ..."

Brringg.

He pulled his phone out of his suit pocket, but he only looked down quickly enough to see the little black heart Chloe had sent him before his eyes went back up, realizing he had already lost Enzo's ugly hat.

"Where'd he go?" Lucca gripped the phone, holding on to the fact that Chloe was safe and no one he didn't trust knew her location. "Where the fuck did he go?"

"Lucca!"

Searching the crowd for the person who boomed out his name, his eyes landed on Dom's hazel ones, finding the source.

This time, the Luciano mob boss only needed to mouth the words, "*Someone got out.*"

THE GRIP he had on her tightened as he pulled her. "We need to go."

Chloe fought against both of their holds, and neither eased their grasp on her, but Chloe had made a promise to Lucca that she wasn't going anywhere without Amo or Vincent, *even if it was one of their father's.*

"Where's Amo?"

"He's helping Vincent get the rest of your friends out the other exit."

The grip on her arm turned rougher, forcing her to take a step away from the theater doors ... But Gia jerked her back.

"Who *is* he?"

Chloe couldn't believe what was happening as she looked at the older Caruso member who held her in a tight vice. He was supposed to be a long-time family friend of Lucca's, but something screamed at her that something wasn't right. "H-he's—"

"Hurry up ... there's no time," she was cut off.

The strength he was exerting on her arm really hurt now, making it even more difficult to pull away.

That's it!

"Well, we're going to *make* time." Chloe refused to be budged despite the fiery pain. "I promised Lucca I wouldn't leave *your* son. Gia and I *will* go back into the theater and go out the way they went."

Vile practically spewed out of his mouth that she'd dare question him. "*You stupid bitch ...*"

Chloe froze at the hateful way he'd spoken to her. Despite the pain that was slowly turning into numbness, she began to struggle against his restraining hold.

Horror filled her when his other hand went to his side to pull a gun out, but all she could think about was her new friend, whom she had just put in this horrible situation.

"Run, Gia!"

"She's going with—"

Gia didn't allow him the opportunity to finish what he was saying. Releasing the grasp she had on Chloe's arm, she grabbed for his gun, turned her body into his and, using her other arm, elbowed him in the nose.

Finding herself unexpectedly released, Chloe's mind only had a second to react to what was happening. She didn't want to endanger her other friends inside of the theater, especially Maria, who was pregnant, yet Vincent was inside and could help.

Gathering her senses as Gia continued to struggle for the gun, Chloe ran to the theater door, flinging it wide open.

"Vincent, help!" she screamed at the top of her lungs, thinking as strategically as she possibly could for everyone's safety. "Maria, get everyone out the exit door!"

Hoping that was enough to make her listen, Chloe quickly ran back to Gia, who now had control of the gun. She was practically using the handle as a battering ram on the assailant's skull while she fought from being strangled.

Knowing Maria would do it if she were here, Chloe went to help Gia, desperately trying to grab at the hands strangling her friend in hopes she could catch a single breath.

"What the hell?" Vincent yelled, shoving her out of the way to attempt to do what Chloe didn't have the muscle to. His baby blues locked on to the man he was fighting off that he no longer recognized ... "Dad?"

TAKE A LUCKY GUESS

"What the fuck are you doing?" Vincent snarled at him.

When his father didn't answer, he yelled at Chloe over his shoulder, "Where's Amo?"

Chloe spoke as fast as she could, trying to fill him in. "I don't know. He was gone when we came out of the bathroom! Vinny grabbed me and told me Lucca sent him, and that it was an emergency!"

Just as she finished getting the words out, she found herself suddenly propelled back when Maria's hand clutched hers from behind in a tight grip.

Standing next to all her friends now, Chloe could see they were in the same amount of shock as she was to what they were seeing.

Lake's eyes were practically as round as saucers. "Why is Gia beating up Vincent's father?"

"I don't know." Chloe shook her head in dismay before pivoting to a pregnant Maria. "I told you to leave."

"Yeah, well, I've never done anything I'm supposed to do." Maria's gaze didn't waver from the trio struggling as she opened her purse and began shouting out orders. "Kat, go check out the men's restroom. Adalyn, go check out the door on the other side of the women's restroom."

"I will." Chloe made her voice just as firm as Maria's, daring anyone to question her. "Elle, get everyone and go."

Elle took one look at her face and knew she was no longer that scarred girl who needed protecting. Grabbing Adalyn and Lake by their arms, she ushered them down the walkway and toward the concession stand.

Proud of herself, Chloe went up to the door that was most likely the cleaning closet, only to find it locked. At the same time, Maria revealed what she kept in her purse.

Taking out a pretty, shiny pistol, Maria walked over in her stilettos to the consigliere and pressed the metal against his forehead.

"*Let. Her. Go,*" the mafia princess ordered lethally.

"Maria, w-what are you doing?" Vinny's face went even redder. Slowly, he let go of Gia and started raising his hands in the air. "Lucca sent me to protect Chloe, likely to protect her from Gia."

Maria, however, didn't remove the gun. "If Gia wanted to take Chloe out, she would have shot her already instead of using it on you."

"Amo's here! He's hurt!"

At Kat's shout, Chloe moved toward the men's restroom, but Maria's voice had her stopping.

"Stay where you are, Chloe," she ordered, not knowing what could await her in the men's bathroom. "Where I can see you."

"What about Amo?" Chloe asked, understanding that Vinny could possibly have an accomplice, but she couldn't help it that she wanted to help her friend.

"Kat, call an ambulance!" Maria yelled, knowing there was nothing they could do for him, anyway.

Seeing Maria had it under control, Gia pulled herself out from under Vinny.

Vincent stood there in complete shock. It felt like the longest he had gone without saying a word.

"You have a phone. Call Lucca," Maria ordered him while her deadly gaze didn't deviate from his father.

Looking up at them all surrounding him, Vinny was smart enough to know there was no talking himself out of this one. "Vincent, *shoot* Maria. If you make that call to Lucca, I'm a dead man."

Slowly, Vincent reached into his suit jacket while Chloe's breath hitched in her throat ...

LUCCA LOOKED DOWN at an unconscious Luciano soldier who lay in the hallway. "How long?"

Quickly checking his pulse, Dom shook his head. "Not sure."

It was obvious the soldier, who had been guarding the door on the outside, was dead, and One-Shot was on the move. They had all been watching the door throughout the night.

"Everyone upstairs," Lucca began instructing only those he trusted, having an idea it could have only happened moments ago. "Sal, I want you on the computers now."

The door cracked open from someone inside wondering what was going on in the hallway. "Everything all rig— oh shit."

Lucca turned cold when he saw Enzo.

Brring.

This time, it wasn't a text but a call, and when he saw Vincent's name, the *real* fear seeped in.

Instinctively knowing nothing good was going to come out of this call, he answered ...

∞

IT WASN'T until she saw the phone in his hand that she could begin to breathe again.

Maria, on the other hand, hadn't bothered to look in Vincent's direction. "Unlike *you*," she hissed, pressing the barrel of the gun deeper into the head of the man she could only assume was One-Shot, "Vincent is loyal to the Caruso family."

Vinny stared at his son as if Vincent had been the one to betray him. "My death will be on your conscience."

"No," Vincent spoke slowly, as if he couldn't believe the words coming out of his mouth. "The only one responsible for your death is *you*. You knew you were a dead man the moment you touched Chloe ... You made your bed. Now fucking *lie. In. It.*"

Chloe had never seen him like this. She wanted to cry at Vincent's shattered expression as he spoke into the phone. Like Adalyn, he lived in his own world, the rest of them being "sometimes annoyed" participants, but now her heart ached for him. Vincent was not only a good person but a good friend.

Rubbing her neck, Gia flexed her shoulder as if it was hurting her. "Are you all right, Chloe?"

"Yes." Chloe dismissed the stinging pain in her arm from Vinny grabbing her, still a bit in shock at seeing how her new friend had reacted like a badass. "Thanks to you."

Concentrating on keeping her gun pointed at Vinny,

Maria sent a questioning glance toward Gia. "Will someone please tell me who the hell she is?"

Good question.

Gia gave a small laugh while she reached at her back to pull out a zip tie from under her loose hoodie. "Allow me to introduce myself." Bending down, she forced Vinny's hands behind his back to restrain him with her zip tie handcuffs that had even Maria raising an appreciative brow at her moves. "I'm Gianna, Chloe's private bodyguard."

What the—

As if she hadn't been shocked enough for one night, Chloe's mouth dropped open. She felt as if Gia had swept her legs out from under her.

Taking a deep breath, Chloe promised herself she wouldn't overreact *until* she heard her fiancé's name out of Gia's mouth after her question.

"Who hired you?"

Able to put the gun away, Maria had to hold her baby bump from laughing so hard, making it clear it wasn't just Gia she was impressed with tonight.

Smiling confidently, the *real* Gianna no longer had to conceal herself ...

"Take a lucky guess."

HIS FATHER'S SON AFTER ALL

His soldiers led One-Shot into the Switzerland warehouse filled with both families. With a hard shove, Drago pushed Vinny to his knees in front of him.

Lucca stared down at the man who had eluded him; a man who, since he was a child, he had thought only had the best interests of the Caruso family at heart. Years upon years they had sought his advice, and each time, they had taken it without hesitation. Vinny had betrayed every single person who stood here today who had been brought to witness his punishment ...

But Lucca's current thoughts were consumed by the person he had betrayed the most.

His own son.

Looking over at Nero, he nodded his head toward the door.

Nero placed his hand on a solemn Vincent's shoulder and nudged him, but he shook his head firmly. Vincent wanted to witness what was about to take place, thought he deserved to more than the rest of them, but there were just some things you didn't need to see ... and his baby blues, more piercing than usual because of the redness and tears he was unable to hide, was one.

Vincent was ready to fight to stay. It wasn't until a bandaged Amo placed his hand on his other shoulder when Vincent finally agreed to leave.

The warehouse went silent as the three friends left and the door was finally closed.

Over the last twenty-four hours, they had learned *how* he had done it. As consigliere, he had been allowed in every room. If his presence in places caught on any cameras, it wasn't unusual, while other times, he went undetected. Vinny had learned how to evade the security cameras by finding out which areas could and could not be seen by memorizing the security screens.

And now, Lucca was able to ask the only question that seared his mind since One-Shot's first kill ...

"Why?"

"Just kill me and get it over with." Vinny lifted his face filled with hatred for all to finally see as he stared at his new boss defiantly. "If you want to ask why ... then ask your father."

That was the thing. *I did.*

"He doesn't know."

Vinny snarled with laughter, "He knows."

All right, then ...

From the shadows, a man strode out to stand in the light. Cigar smoke filled the air as Dante came closer to stand next to his son.

"I don't." Dante stepped up to stand over what was had been his best friend. "We were raised side by side—you, Enzo, and me—and I never *once, ever* doubted your loyalty."

Vinny's hatred for Dante could no longer be masked,

making them all wonder how he had been able to hide it so well for so many years, or worse ... they all managed to miss it.

"How easy you forget *Emilia*."

A pained expression crossed Dante's face. "I've never forgotten Emilia."

Emilia? Lucca had never heard that name spoken before, at least not in his presence.

Vinny lunged for Dante, but his father didn't waiver. He remained still as stone as Drago dragged Vinny back to his knees.

"Do not *dare* speak my *sister's* name," he hissed. His usual regal tone as consigliere was gone. "When your father arranged yours and Emilia's marriage, you refused to marry her the day before the wedding. She was *humiliated*."

Dante angrily shook his head down at him. "That's not true, Vinny, and you know it. You know exactly why I refused to marry her. I even had your father's permission to break it and pull out of the wedding."

"My father listened to Emilia's pleas. I told him not to." Vinny's eyes no longer hid his true feelings of jealousy as he stared at Dante. "I knew who you *really* wanted."

"Emilia came to me, *begging* the night before our wedding not to make her go through with the ceremony. She told me her heart belonged to the church and what her true calling was. She threatened to kill herself if we married." Dante looked down at him in disbelief that he could see the past so differently than how it had happened. "Is that what you would have preferred? A dead sister over one who wanted to be a nun? I thought a man of your devotedness could understand that, Vinny."

"Emilia would have *never* harmed herself. She would have never committed that *sin*." Vinny shook his head knowingly. "Instead, you took the bride *I* had been promised."

"I asked you before I accepted the arrangement. You're the one who told me to go through with it. If you had wanted Melissa, I wouldn't have agreed to our marriage." Dante's voice was now incapable of hatred as he spoke of his dead wife. "I loved Melissa more than life itself, but our love grew with time, like in any arranged marriage."

"How was I supposed to say no to our fathers?" Vinny's voice was filled with loathing after having to listen to him. "To you? My father was *your* father's consigliere. To continue our lineage as the Carusos' advisors was the source of our family's pride. I would have been blamed if I had taken Melissa and you retaliated by making Enzo your consigliere. I couldn't take that chance. Instead, I had to fucking watch her fall in love with you and give you the children who should have been *mine*."

"You had a child." Dante chewed on his cigar angrily. "Vincent."

Vinny gave a snort of sarcasm. "Vincent is no Lucca."

Lucca held no sympathy for him. Even though his son was irritating at times ... "Vincent is a far better man than you. He would *never* betray Nero and Amo the way *you* have."

"You took what was meant to be mine," Vinny hissed before he smiled. "I bided my time ... before I repaid in kind. I held my vengeance until I knew it would hurt the most."

When Dante went for him, Lucca had to put out a staying arm to keep him in place.

He was finally able to understand all he needed to know. Once Lucca had taken Lucifer out of the picture, Vinny was able to suggest the two family bloodlines mix only so a Luciano could be blamed for his crimes. Choosing Dominic to take the fall was the smartest, as not only was he Lucifer's heir who would seek revenge for his father, but Dom had only one method of killing. There was only one thing Vinny didn't take into account—that Lucca had known all there was to know about Dominic Luciano. That not only would he never seek revenge for his father's death, but he would never shoot a man through the back of the head if he could help it.

Having the last piece of the puzzle, Lucca was just as tired as his father of waiting. "I've heard everything I want to hear." Vinny had confessed to his disloyalty, and it was time for him to earn his penitence. "Enzo is to discuss with you how much he appreciated his son's stay in the hospital."

Drago lifted Vinny using the back of his suit, jerking him to face the man who was supposed to be one of his best friends.

Taking his hat off, Enzo was able to show his own hatred before his fist reared back to strike Vinny.

Crazy laughter poured out of Vinny's mouth instead of a pain-filled scream. The sound had Enzo looking at Dante instead of hitting Vinny again.

Lucca had just placed a cigarette to his lips when Vinny spat out blood at his and Dante's feet before the next words out of his mouth sent chills up everyone's spines.

"I made sure Melissa saw me pull the trigger."

Dante swayed, his words barely audible. "You're lying."

"Am I?" His blood-stained smile said otherwise.

Lucca snapped his lighter closed before he even managed to light the end. The stick fell to the ground with the first word he spoke. "Lucifer killed my mother."

"I let him take the glory," Vinny began to brag, "but it was *my* bullet that ended her life."

Dante gave a howl of pain, jerking Vinny free from Drago.

No! Lucca tried to pull his father away, to get him to see reason. "He wants you to kill him fast. Don't let him goad you."

"Let go of me, Lucca. I know what he's fucking doing," Dante growled at his son.

He witnessed true pain in his father's icy eyes. Melissa might have been his mother, but she was Dante's wife first ...

So, he let him go.

Suddenly, Dante grabbed Vinny by the throat, squeezing until Vinny went back to his knees. "You fucking coward. How did you fucking hide how big of a pussy you are so well? It didn't take much courage to kill a gentle woman who wouldn't harm a fly, nor shoot someone when you can't be seen! You're a fucking weasel to hide in the middle of the night to plant a fucking bomb!"

Finally, Dante released his grip around Vinny's throat when he started to turn purple, leaving him gasping for air. Taking the cigar out of his mouth, Dante raised it high in the air.

"An *eye* for an *eye*."

Drago held Vinny's head steady as Dante stabbed the smoldering tip of the cigar into Vinny's left eye.

Allowing Vinny only one agonizing scream, Dante squeezed his airway again as he left the cigar in the socket.

"Drago, knife," Dante ordered.

When Drago looked at him for permission, Lucca shook his head. Then he slowly stepped forward. Pulling out his own knife, he gave his father a knowing nod.

Dante allowed Vinny another scream, using the opportunity to hold Vinny's mouth open. "A lying tongue, for the betraying lies you told."

Lucca gripped the knife and cut out Vinny's tongue, placing the flesh in the liar's front suit pocket.

The gurgling sounds coming from Vinny showed them all he was still very much alive.

Lucca might have said One-Shot was his for the taking, but he held out the bloody knife to his father.

Taking it, Dante screamed down at Vinny, "And a heart for the broken heart you ripped out of me." He stabbed the knife down into his old friend's chest, carving Vinny's heart out, ripping it right out of his body, and giving Lucca a newfound respect for his father as he watched.

Heart in his hand, Dante threw it to the ground and began smashing it under his shoe, over ... and over ... and over again ...

"Dad." Lucca couldn't remember the last time he had called him that, but somehow, it seemed appropriate. "He's dead."

As if Dante couldn't hear, he started kicking Vinny's dead body, and when Sal moved to stop him, Lucca shook his head. He could understand his father's rage. Chloe was right; Dante had loved his mother very much, and it was the one thing Lucca had always known to be true. The grief Dante had bottled up and hid from anyone watching his pain after his wife's death was finally set free on the man responsible for killing her.

It wasn't until several minutes later when Dante let the knife fall to the ground and took off his suit jacket. The outside a bloody mess, he used the inside to wipe his blood-covered face.

"You couldn't save anything for us?" Lucca asked wryly

as he saw Dante's reasoning return as he flung his coat over the gory body.

"No." Dante stared at him, then at Sal, at Drago, and all of the other men he used to order around. "I want you all to be able to look Vincent in the eye in the years to come."

It was a kind sentiment from the man who had once been the head of this family.

Lucca came to two realizations as he looked at his predecessor ...

That not only was Dante one of their greatest Dons in history, but he was his father's son *after all.*

LOOSE ENDS

Freshly washed and bathed, Lucifer sat down at the table that had been set up for him in his cell. When he reached to the other side of the table for the plate, his fingertips stopped just a millimeter away from the thing he desired as it sat barely out of reach.

"Patience," Lucca heeded, picking up the knife and fork to begin cutting the warm steak.

The devilish eyes darted between the delicious-looking meal and the man sitting across from him with anticipation. Licking his lips, he finally asked, "What's the occasion?"

Raising his fork, Lucca took a bite of a smaller piece, making sure it still tasted like perfection before he placed the utensils back down in front of him to where only he could reach. "My wedding's coming up."

"Congratulations."

The hostility and jealousy over Chloe in his tone no longer affected Lucca. It was the same tone Vinny had used toward his father, and in the end, Dante and he ... had *won*.

Finally, Lucca slid the plate in front of him, and for the first time, Lucifer didn't inhale the food like a starved dog.

He picked up a single piece at a time with his clean fingers to place them in his mouth. He would savor it, chewing it slowly before it slid down his throat.

He was halfway through the large steak when he realized just how good it actually tasted. "Where did you get this from? *Carbone?*"

"No." While Lucca appreciated the sentiment, even the most expensive Italian steakhouse in Kansas City couldn't compare. "I prepared it."

Lucifer chewed even slower then swallowed with relief showing in his eyes.

"It's not poisoned," Lucca promised, dashing away any of his hopes.

His captive, while agitated, could at least appreciate what he was given as he picked up another piece. "Man of many talents, I see."

A compliment was not what Lucca had come here to seek.

"So," Lucifer began, knowing he wasn't getting the royal treatment just because Lucca was getting married, "what has *really* happened for me to deserve this pleasure?"

Lucca stayed silent, knowing the guessing games were what kept Lucifer sane these days.

"Ah!" Lucifer's face lit up with a wicked smile. "You found out it was Vinny Vitale all along."

There were two questions Lucca had for him, and he was pretty sure they both led to the same answer.

"How did you know it was him?"

"No one hated your father more than me." In fact, Lucifer hated him so much he couldn't even bring himself to say Dante's name at the moment. "*Except* ... for Vinny."

Watching him swallow down another piece of steak, Lucca knew he wasn't finished blabbing.

"Emilia was pretty, *but come on*; she was no comparison to Melissa." Lucifer looked up from the remaining pieces of steak and at him appreciatively. "I, for one, could understand his envy."

Lucca was beginning to see the pattern. Thrones weren't the only thing every one thirsted for, but for a wife strong enough to stand beside them, and for the son who could possess it. If there was one thing Lucca understood, it was that ... *every throne comes with a price.*

He carefully scrutinized the devil's face to see his reaction to his next question. "Why did you tell us that you killed her?"

Mid-swallow, Lucifer appeared to be caught off guard before he answered. "Because he was too pussy to take the credit."

When Lucca only continued to stare back, Lucifer's face fell for a brief moment, revealing the truth of it all. "I had no *real* great achievement I could claim, anyway, so I claimed the one you were convinced I committed."

"But you did." Lucca felt anger rising in him again for Lucifer saying he had no great achievement to claim. "Pity you'll never get to see it."

"What?" Lucifer asked with hope in his dead eyes.

Lucca, however, didn't want him to go to his grave proud and knowing that Dominic had restored the Luciano name to the greatness it had once been.

"You'll never know," Lucca promised. *At least, not from me.*

Ignoring the last two bites, Lucifer suddenly picked up the plate and tried to smash it but found it to be plastic when it didn't break.

Proud he had thought of that, Lucca smiled and carefully took everything back out of the room. It wasn't that he thought Lucifer would have used it as a weapon against him; he'd feared Lucifer would have used it on himself.

Returning to the concrete cell, Lucca truly looked at Lucifer this time. Now that the man before him was clean, he was able to see the amount of damage he had inflicted on him. The dirt and grime had covered his scars and the pounds of flesh he had taken from him for his crimes. With every scar he had given Chloe, he had repaid in kind and then some, making Lucifer Luciano unrecognizable. And his time in this cell had not been kind. With him about to marry Chloe, it was time he *finally* moved on ...

"This is the last time you'll ever see me, Lucifer." Lucca made him another grave promise. "The next person who comes to visit you ... *will be your maker.*"

The sheer fear in Lucifer's eyes grew, but Lucca couldn't see it as he had already walked away.

"How long will that be?" the devil screamed at his back, his emotions warring between terror and anger.

When Lucca slid the heavy metal door closed for his final time, there was no compassion in his cold voice. "When he's ready."

HER DRIVER PULLED into the front of the Casino Hotel. When he exited the car, Maria looked up at the roof to see a million little lights that looked like stars as she waited for the door to her pearlescent Rolls Royce to open.

"Thanks, Vic." She smiled at the big man who had opened the door for her as she slid out. Maria refused to call him by the name Blue Park had given him as Big Vic.

As he tipped his expensive hat, Maria walked by, leaving him there until her return.

Entering and walking through the casino, she went up the elevator before reaching the door of the war-room they continued to use for meetings.

Sending the door swinging open, the new consigliere entered in an all-white women's suit she'd paired with nude pumps. She would definitely be returning to the designer store to get a smaller size after she had her baby.

"Hello, boys."

The sea of black-suited men's mouths dropped to the floor. The only ones who didn't were the boss and his temporary underboss, Enzo.

"I've been told *black* isn't my color."

THE SLIDING of the partition had Lucca looking through the ornate window.

"Forgive me, Father, for I have sinned. It has been a long time since my last confession."

The shadow on the other side slightly moved, knowing who sat on the other side of the partition by that dark voice. "Yes, my son?"

"Did you know Emilia?"

He had come to ask only for a favor, so why was it he was asking a question about a past that no longer served a purpose?

The shadowed man sat there in silence.

"Emilia *Vitale*?" he clarified, but Lucca was pretty sure that the figure had known exactly who he was talking about the first time.

"I—" The priest cleared his dry throat. "I do."

"Can you tell me about her?"

"Well ..." The priest was well aware Lucca wasn't here

to speak to him as a son of God but as the King of Kansas City. "What would you like to know?"

"Is she still alive?" he asked, supposing what he wanted was to tie up loose ends.

"Yes." It was obvious, even though a wall separated them, that the priest was uncomfortable answering, but knowing who was asking the questions had him doing so honestly. "She still cares for children at the very first orphanage she went to after she spoke her vows."

Was it relief overcoming him?

"So ... she is a nun?"

"Yes," the priest confirmed, growing nervous. "May I ask *why* you are asking me this, Lucca?"

Content with that information, Lucca was finally able to let the past *go*.

"It no longer matters." When the shadow nervously shifted, Lucca continued, "Don't worry, Father; I have no intention of murdering a nun."

He heard a quick, quiet prayer on the other side. Then there was calmness in the priest's voice when it returned. "Then, is there something else I can help you with, my son?"

"There is." Lucca came to finally ask the favor. "Would you marry my fiancée and me?"

Warmth exuded in his words, as the father said, "Of course. Your mother would be very proud, Lucca. The church—"

"Not here, Father," Lucca politely stopped him. "At our home."

"Lucca ..." he warned, "you know, as a man of the faith, there are rules I must follow. Getting authorization for a wedding outside of the church is few and far between."

"I know that," Lucca gritted out. Having to remind

himself to stay calm, he tried again. "I was hoping you didn't *need* their authorization."

The priest thought for several moments before answering, "I don't think I can do that, Lucca."

He got up and left the confessional. Not even bothering to close the wooden door, Lucca began walking out of the church, planning on never returning.

"Lucca," the priest called out, hoping to change his mind. "Your mother would be very happy to see you married here."

At the mention of his mother, Lucca spun on his heel to face him. "Forgive me, Father, but my mother isn't here." He looked around at the cathedral that his mother had dragged him to, but he didn't feel any connection to it ... It was only to the priest who spoke to his mother every Sunday that he did. "She's with me at home, where the flowers she taught me how to grow are."

WHERE THE FLOWERS GROW

Unable to stop herself, Chloe snuck a peek of the back garden, at the guests waiting for the wedding to begin. Before she could count how many guests there were, Maria slid the curtain closed, putting them out of sight but not out of mind. Chloe still knew there were a lot of people waiting for her entrance.

"Please, ladies ..." Maria snapped her manicured fingers, breaking up the excited chatter of Chloe's bridesmaids. "It's time for us to get in position."

Oh no.

Elle, seeing she was frozen in fear, linked her arm with hers and moved her away from the opened French doors that were curtained for their reveal, to the back of the line, where her bridesmaids were forming. "You've got this."

However, her best friend's encouraging words didn't ease her queasy stomach.

"No, I don't," Chloe whispered back, trying to keep the little bit of food she could eat today in her stomach. "I *really* don't."

"*Yes. You. Do,*" Elle reassured her, bringing them to a stop at the end of the line.

"I'm going to trip."

Elle chuckled, and with the squeeze of her arm, she let go, knowing her best friend's true strength. "No, you're not."

Oh God ... "I'm going to throw up," she warned, placing a hand over her stomach.

Maria linked her arm with the arm Elle had just released. "If you do, just make sure you turn your head so none of it hits me." Patting down her styled blonde locks, she gave her a threatening glance. "I look too good to be covered in vomit."

Chloe felt her lips tremble in laughter at the thought of Maria looking anything but magnificent, even covered in vomit. The thought eased her nerves until the panic set in when the line started moving. She didn't budge when Maria tried to propel her forward, unable to force her feet to move.

What's happening? What am I doing? This is crazy! Am I really about to get marri—

"If you don't start moving, Lucca is going to think you don't want to marry him." Maria's usual overly sweet tone disappeared. "Now, do you want to ruin the happiest day of my brother's life?"

No. She sighed. Chloe didn't want to spoil Lucca's day, or hers, or the whole world's, for that matter, if she didn't walk down that aisle to where the flowers grow.

Holding on to Maria's arm for dear life, she started walking, feeling like she was about to—

"It's going to be hard to give my protégé away. Just remember everything I taught you," Maria began whispering to her as they headed for the curtained French doors. "Always make him do the dishes after dinner—"

With each step, Maria gave her another piece of advice.

"—keep him on his toes—"

Another step.

"—and pretend he forgot something important and make him beg for forgiveness."

One more step.

"When you do get mad at him, order takeout. It'll cut him to his soul."

Tears already brimming her eyes as they reached the curtained door, Chloe hugged Maria and placed a kiss on her cheek before they had to walk through it. "Thank you, Maria. After my parents ..." She trailed off as she thought about her father and mother, who had died in a tragic gas explosion not that long ago. Even though they had never truly cared for her like they should have, there was still a little sadness that her parents weren't here. "You've just made it easier for me to get through the day without any family."

"You've *always* been a member of the Caruso family, Chloe." Maria smiled ever so sweetly then winked. "This is just going to make it official."

"That's right," a deep voice said from behind her.

Turning, she stared up at Lucca's father.

It wasn't until Dante got a nod of approval from Maria that he held out an arm. "Chloe, would you give me the honor of righting a wrong by being able to walk *one* of my daughters down the aisle?"

Overwhelmed with joy that he'd asked, she still looked at Maria for her approval.

Maria was still smiling but now with tears in her eyes. There was no jealousy showing in them, only complete self-lessness and happiness before Maria walked through the curtain and down the aisle to her place.

Smiling with glossy eyes of her own, Chloe took her soon-to-be father-in-law's strong arm. "Of course."

"Thank you," Dante uttered hoarsely, patting her hand and giving her all his strength.

And with that, Chloe took a final deep breath, growing worried she might not live up to Lucca's expectations of what he wanted her to look like on their wedding day until ...

∞

WHEN THE CURTAIN OPENED, Lucca's blue-green eyes met the precious gray ones he loved with all of his heart since the moment he had first seen her.

There were no words to describe Chloe's beauty. There was nothing like her on this earth that could compare. She was as exquisite as she was rare. Her porcelain skin; long, silky black hair; and the scars she no longer tried to hide were a testament to that fact. Somehow, though, it was her inner beauty that was her most alluring of features.

Every day, he was amazed at her beauty, but today, with the sun shining brightly and the garden in full bloom as she walked toward him down the aisle, she looked ethereal. The dress she had chosen to marry him in was as exquisite as she was, but it was the never-ending veil covered in a million white roses that had his eyes going misty.

He could feel his mother here as he looked at her, as he smelled the flowers, as he felt the wind touch his skin, as he looked at the emerald-green dresses and accents Chloe had chosen to match his mother's eyes. Like the priest who stood behind him had said she would be, *she is proud.*

His father didn't hide his pride, either, as he went to give away whom Lucca would call his fiancée for the last time, letting not only his son but the family know that Dante gave his full approval.

When a breathtakingly beautiful Chloe approached the gazebo where they had first met, Lucca smiled as he held out his hand for her to take. They were about to say the most important two words they'd say in their entire lives to each other, but there were two important ones that had started it all ...

"Hey, darlin'."

MEANT TO BE

Their wedding had been absolutely beautiful, and she couldn't be happier with how it had gone. She was glad she hadn't changed a thing or made it smaller since they had gotten to share their love with all their family and friends. But, now that it was over, Chloe couldn't understand why she was so nervous as she stood in the bathroom alone. It wasn't like they hadn't had sex before ... Maybe it was because, in the week they had moved into the Caruso family home after Dante had gifted them the house as a wedding present, Lucca had slept in his parents' old bedroom while she had stayed in his old room.

As she'd slept alone, she'd been afraid some of her old nightmares would make a return appearance, but they hadn't. She had felt safe and secure in the bed without Lucca there, and on the third day of sleeping alone, she had come to the awareness that she was no longer the terrified teenager, afraid of her own shadow. She was an adult who understood—as much as she didn't want to—that evil could take place during the night *and the day*.

She might not be scared of nightmares anymore, but what she had become afraid of, and she couldn't fathom why, was the fragility of life itself. Ever since Lucca had expressed God wouldn't have a place for him in heaven, all she could think about was him believing he was without redemption.

There was something he didn't know, and that was the boogieman had a heart after all.

In the bathroom, she shook her head at herself as she put on the sheer, frilly negligée Elle had gifted her at her bachelorette party. Then she opened the door, expecting her wide-awake husband, but found Lucca sound asleep. In shock and disbelief he could possibly fall asleep early on their wedding night, she moved to the bed, about to wake him, but when she glanced at the clock on the nightstand, she realized it was her fault he had fallen sleep. She had been in the bathroom too long.

Damn.

She got up to turn off the light and hoped she wouldn't trip over something in the unfamiliar bedroom, but when she flipped the switch, Chloe stood in stunned delight at the cast of a soft, warm glow across the ceiling.

"Do you like it?" Lucca asked from the bed.

"I love it." She looked up in awe as she made her way to the bed and slid under the blankets when he pulled the covers back for her. "I thought you were asleep."

"On my wedding night?" Lucca slid his hand over her belly to reach for her hip, pulling her to his chest. "Nero, Vincent, and Dom would never let me live it down."

Curling into his warm body, she pressed a kiss to his tanned cheek. "They wouldn't say anything." Chloe almost snorted at the thought. *Well* ... "At least not within your hearing. Besides, how would they know?"

"Because *you* would tell one of the girls, and from there, it would all fucking go downhill."

An offended Chloe's jaw dropped. "I would not."

But Lucca knew his new wife too well. "You would."

"Be careful, you're coming dangerously close to starting a fight on our wedding night," she warned, giving him the glare that was still a work in progress. "And I haven't totally forgiven you for not telling me you had hired Gia to be my bodyguard."

"You're the one who wanted Professor Grabby Hands back *and* didn't want any of the men accompanying you into the restroom," Lucca reminded her without an ounce of remorse. "So, I *whacked* two birds with one stone."

Chloe chuckled, but then a small part of her happiness suddenly dimmed. "I talked to Vincent this evening before we left. I didn't mention his father." She swallowed hard, her mind going back to the evil look that had been in Vinny's eyes and the desolate one in his son's. "How's he doing?"

Lucca thought for a moment. "He's ... *adjusting.*"

She hoped it wouldn't take long, and even though he could be a little much at times, she missed Vincent. He seemed so distant, but ... *maybe he is thinking about where he could be?*

"I was so relieved you didn't fire Drago when Vinny escaped on the way to the police station. I told Kat you wouldn't. I didn't want her worried. You don't think Vinny might try to hurt one of us again, though, do you?"

"No." He cleared his throat before continuing, "I'm sure he's somewhere *warm* and far, *far* away from here, and I'm content with that."

"Me, too." Chloe nodded, certain that must be the truth.

Lucca had always told her in the beginning that he'd never lie to her.

"Mrs. Caruso ..." he purred out her new name, getting her back to the importance of the day, "there is a lot of talking going on and no sex."

At Lucca's hard kiss, she raised her arms to embrace him, only to find herself grasping at air. "Where are you going?"

"You still seem stressed from the wedding." The smoldering look on Lucca's face had her breath catching when he returned and jerked the covers to the foot of the bed. Taking his time, he removed her flimsy gown to stare down at her body from where he stood at the edge of the bed, as if he weren't already familiar with every curve and bump.

"How do you always make me feel as if I'm beautiful?" she asked breathlessly, staring up at him.

"Because you are," he assured her, flicking open his Zippo lighter that he had retrieved.

She frowned. *He's going to smoke?* He hadn't smoked around her at all lately, but at that thought, she watched him take the silver lid off a short glass candle and light the wick. It wasn't long before the spicy scent filled the air and mixed with Lucca's minty fresh one, creating ice and fire.

"Lie down," he commanded.

Unquestioningly, she obeyed his order, and her whole body tingled as she watched Lucca hold the candle high above her.

"Don't be afraid, darlin'."

"I'm not," she assured him. The fear of pain no longer lived in her as she trustingly waited for what he would do next. In that moment, while she waited for what would come, she realized that loving Lucca was like a four-alarm fire—sometimes, there was no escape.

He dipped two fingers into the candle then pulled them out to rub what she thought was hot wax between them. Seemingly satisfied, he then slowly tipped the candle over, spilling a slim stream from the base of her throat to her mound. It was warm but not unbearably ...

Touching it gingerly, Chloe realized it was oil.

Lucca climbed back onto the bed to spread her thighs. Seductively, he started massaging the oil into her skin. He didn't miss an inch—her neck, hands, arms, stomach, legs, feet ... *oh, the feet* ... except ... anything *really* important.

He had only traced the curve of her breast, skimmed above her bikini line ... to make it even more torturous. The Lucca she was used to had faded into non-existence. The man tormenting her with his skilled hands was the boogie-man, watching his victim squirm for more.

"Lucca ... please."

But her pleas went unheard as he relit the candle. When he tested the warmth again before tipping it, this time, she held her breath, silently praying the oil would go where she wanted it to.

"Lucca!" Chloe couldn't help the scream of frustration when he trailed the oil between her breasts.

"Do you want something, darlin'?" Lucca smiled sinisterly before he surrounded a pink nipple with his mouth.

The *old* Chloe would have lain there and let Lucca have his way until he would let her come. The *new* Chloe, however, had had enough.

Scooping some of the oil onto her fingers, she started massaging it onto his dick. She couldn't help but smile at him mischievously when his hungry eyes caught hers in surprise. Using her own knowledge of Lucca's likes, she had the boogieman trembling within minutes.

Finally at his entrance inside of her, she gave a satisfied

moan of pure pleasure, but Chloe wasn't about to lose the ground she had just earned. Matching his movements, she returned every caress and push he gave her.

Most of the time, she had felt inexperienced when they made love, but tonight, they became the lovers they were *meant to be ... over* and *over* again until exhaustion overtook them, leaving them tangled in each other's arms.

Trailing fingertips traveled down her spine, waking her.

"Ready for a shower?"

"No. You go ahead," she mumbled groggily.

"Sorry, we're not going to sleep in this oil." Getting off the bed, a particular Lucca lifted her into his arms to carry her into the shower, letting the water grow warm before walking inside. Chloe let him do all the work of washing them, rubbing her back against his chest as she did her best to stay awake.

"I don't know why I'm so sleepy. That's all I did all this week." She yawned widely. "I'm going to order some vitamins. That should help."

"Don't order them until your gyno tells you which ones to take," Lucca advised.

Psht—

"I'm not going to my gyno because I'm tired." *Men, they really don't know anything.* "If the vitamins don't work, I'll go to my *regular* doctor," Chloe informed him, but then she became worried and turned to face him. "You don't think I could be sick, do you? I can't be sick right now. Finals are coming u—"

"I don't think you're sick, darlin'," he assured her, soothing her small worries only to replace them with a bigger one. "You're pregnant."

What?

"No, I'm not ... I'd know ..." *Right?*

Leaning down, he placed a kiss on the scar that reached her cheek. "Chloe, you're pregnant."

Nope, no way. She shook her head confidently, counting back to when she'd had her last period ...

Then recounting again ....

Until she finally came to the realization ...

Oh shit.

"I-I'm going to have a baby?"

When she finally realized the thing Lucca had known for a while now, he lifted her chin high to correct her. "*We're* going to have a baby."

He was about to capture her mouth with his but was stopped when Chloe placed her fingers over his lips. It was a move he was certain his sister had taught her, making him regret making her his consigliere.

"As the mother of your child, I need to know the truth."

Lucca was already certain he wasn't going to like what she was about to ask.

"Did you *whack* Vinny?"

"I swear *I* didn't kill him ..." he promised without missing a beat while he looked her directly in the eyes. Turned out his father had not only saved him from being unable to look into his soldier's eyes, but his new wife's. "Nor did *I order* him to be."

It *was* the complete and honest truth. Like he'd said, he would never lie to her. He wasn't the one who had ripped Vinny's heart out.

When she threw her arms around his neck in profound relief, he didn't feel bad. If there was anything Lucca had done from the beginning with her, it was showing her his true self. But there were just some things you were better off *not* knowing … Especially when you were married and wanted it to be *happily*.

"I don't think I could have looked at Vincent and Lake if you had." She placed a tender kiss on his lips. "I love you *so* much."

Lucca smiled sweetly. As a new husband, he had to learn a few tricks from his sister, too. "I love you, too, darlin'."

They got out of the shower and dried each other off.

"Lucca." Chloe pulled on a warm bathrobe. "About my parents—"

"Brush your hair, darlin'," Lucca quickly cut off what she was about to say with a kiss. "I'll go make us some chili."

I mean, what the fuck did you expect? You didn't open this book because you thought I was a hero. You opened it because …

I'm the fucking boogieman.

EPILOGUE ONE

SOMETIME IN THE VERY NEAR FUTURE...

The jelly that was being smeared on her belly was cold. Lucca squeezed her hand tightly, making her forget about it until her body adjusted as the doctor smeared it in with her tool.

Both Chloe and Lucca tried their best to make out the fuzzy black and white screen, but they had no idea what they were looking at. All they could see was what appeared to be a little jellybean.

"Congratulations." Dr. Sanderson looked at them with a smile.

And that was when they noticed the other little jellybean sitting beside it.

"You're having twins!"

As she walked downstairs from the bedroom with a waddle, Chloe saw Gia watching *Ninja Warrior* and eating a bag of chips.

"How much longer before Drago gets here?"

"He just texted. Traffic is back-to-back. It's going to take him another thirty minutes."

Chloe rubbed the small of her back. The ache had been intermediate for the last several days. She figured it was from how big her belly had grown carrying two babies instead of one. Even though her mother had been a twin, she never, in a million years, would have thought she would be having them.

"My appointment is in twenty minutes, and Dr. Sanderson is working me in because of my back hurting. If I'm late, she might not see me."

Closing the bag of chips, Gia gave her an ironic roll of her eyes. "The doc would stay four hours late to see you."

"Maybe, but I still don't want to inconvenience her," Chloe said firmly with her back aching a bit more. "Text Drago and tell him he can meet us at the doctor office. I can drive back with him."

"Lucca won't be happy ..." Gia tried to get her to reconsider with a hint of fear in her voice. "The only vehicle we have available is my car, and he told us both you were only to drive with Drago in his boat."

Chloe put her hands on her hips. "I'd rather listen to Lucca's lecture than be late."

"That's easy for you to say. He'll fire me," she mumbled but finally agreed.

"He won't fire you." Opening the door, Chloe waved her outside. "He might *threaten* to, but I won't let him."

Besides, who else was going to be able to take her to the bathroom? There was no going back to a man being her bodyguard.

When she opened the passenger side door, a still reluctant Gia pleaded, "At least get in the back seat and sit in the middle."

Since Gia was doing her a favor by jeopardizing her job, Chloe managed to slide into the back seat. Buckling her seat belt, she tried not to wince as another pain struck her back. If not for the increasing frequency of the pain, she would have waited for Drago, but not wanting to alarm Gia, she kept silent about the pain.

As they drove, Chloe realized that Gia didn't merge onto the lane that would take them to the interstate. "You're going the long way. The interstate will be much faster."

Gia turned on the blinker. "Lucca is going to *kill* me."

"No, he won't," she assured her.

Chloe was reassured herself that she had made the right choice for directing Gia to the interstate since there weren't many cars traveling in the direction they were going. She texted Elle that she was on the way to the doctor's office then looked up to see how far they were from their exit when she saw a car coming toward them, heading in the wrong direction.

"Gia ..." Chloe unconsciously dropped her cell phone to grab her stomach.

"I see it. Hold on!"

"WHERE THE FUCK IS MY WIFE!"

Chloe gave the doctor examining her an embarrassed smile when the curtain was pulled back to reveal her husband. And boy, was he livid.

"Lucca, calm down," she tried to placate her husband as he strode into the curtained-off area. "I'm fine, see? There isn't a scratch on me."

He scanned her quickly before his glare returned to the person in the white coat. "Why hasn't she been moved to a private room?"

The young female intern, who had only walked in moments ago, tried to maintain her professionalism, but Chloe could see the fear in her eyes, just like she could see it in Gia, who was trying her best to blend into the privacy curtain behind her.

"Y-You're Mrs. Caruso's husband?"

"Yes," Lucca gritted out. "Now, *why* hasn't my wife been taken to a private room?"

"As far as we can tell, your wife was unhurt in the accident. The woman who brought her in demanded that your wife be checked out thoroughly. I totally agree with her. With your wife being pregnant, we want to use an over-abundance of caution to protect the health of the mother and children. All the tests are readily available in the ER, and the results will be expedited, as opposed to if she were to be moved to a private room."

Chloe could see calmness overtake Lucca at the doctor's serious attitude toward her health.

"Your wife was just telling me that she had been experiencing back pain, which is why she was enroute to her doctor's office."

Chloe found it difficult to meet his blue-green gaze that had only just started to calm.

"Which is news to me." His wry tone told he was, in fact, no longer calm.

"I didn't want to worry you."

The doctor took her vitals, temporarily blocking Lucca from her view.

"You think it's much better for me to find out this way?"

Chloe tilted her head to see her husband as the doctor

pushed a button on a machine that made the cuff around her arm start tightening.

"I didn't expect to get in a car accident. There was a wrong-way driv—"

"Chloe, I need you to lie back on the bed," the doctor interrupted them.

Doing so, Chloe watched the doctor put her stethoscope into her ears. Her hands spread over her baby bump when she saw the growing concern in the nurse's eyes, who was watching the same machines the doctor was.

She started to become afraid something was wrong when a wave of dizziness hit her.

"Get a crash cart, stat!" the doctor ordered.

"Is something wrong ...?"

Agonizing pain hit her with so much force Chloe couldn't fight the dizziness to actually place where the pain was coming from.

Fearful, she searched for Lucca, needing him to hold on to her to keep her from falling. She was in too much pain to realize she was lying down. When she saw he was just as scared as she was, her gray eyes clung to his precious jeweled ones in fear.

"Lucc—"

Excruciating pain prevented her from forming the words that she so desperately wanted to tell him before darkness hit her with a ruthless speed that was faster than her ability to get the words out.

Chloe had watched enough movies to know what the floating sensation she was experiencing meant ...

She wasn't going to get to tell Lucca she loved him one more time.

And she was never going to get to hold her babies.

At the thought of her children, Chloe began screaming

for them to save her babies. Over and over, she screamed until, with a rush of air, she found herself standing on the edge of a cliff. Terrified she would fall, Chloe stood paralyzed with terror that a sudden gust of wind would send her over the edge.

An unexpected sound had her turning around to see a large dragon rushing right toward her. With the dragon charging, Chloe forgot she was standing on the edge of a cliff and fell backward, staring up at the sky above her. She was going to die *twice* in the same day.

Closing her eyes, she prayed the pain would be brief when she landed below, but her eyes sprung open when she felt talons grip her sides. The dragon was flying, carrying her clutched protectively in its claws.

She was helpless. All she could do was stare at the flying dragon holding her, expecting at any moment to plunge to her death or be ripped apart by the massive mouth.

Terrified with immobilizing fear, it took her a moment to understand that the dragon was *whispering* to her ...

With each hum of its voice, the fear slowly left her body and turned into reassurance at the words of the mythical beast. Even when it released her from its talons, Chloe wasn't afraid as she started falling again ... falling back into the darkness that had carried her here.

Voices penetrated the darkness that was trying to keep her submerged.

"Chloe, darlin' ..." Lucca's raspy voice had her fighting to lift her eyelids. "I'm not going to see our daughters until we can see them together. Melissa and Emilia are crying for their mom."

Hearing herself being called *mom* had Chloe finally lifting her weighted eyelids.

My babies—

"Are they okay?"

Lucca, who was holding her hand, lowered his head to the bed at her voice. She could feel the bed shaking with his relieved sobs.

Clasping his hand tighter in hers, she stared at her exhausted husband. "Is anything wrong with our babies?"

Lucca raised his head. His eyes were so piercingly blue-green from his tears. "Our daughters are healthy, waiting to meet their mother."

Relief flooded her as she stared at the glass walls surrounding her. "What happened?"

"Your heart ..." He sobbed. After giving himself a moment to pull himself together, he was able to tell her what the doctors had said and everything she had missed while she was gone. "You have a congenital birth defect. Your heart couldn't hold up to the strain any longer." Tears continued to spill onto his cheeks, still unbelieving of the news. "You were taken to emergency surgery, where they repaired your heart and performed a C-section."

The hand that held hers grasped tighter, still afraid she might leave him.

"I came so close to losing you." His voice hoarse with emotion, he made her an oath. "Never again. No more children."

He had lost his mother suddenly, and now he had almost lost her in the blink of an eye, and there wasn't a damn thing he could do about it. The only thing he could do would mean he would never have a son.

"Oh, Lucca ... there's nothing to be afraid of." Chloe smiled weakly at him, remembering the magnificent sight she had seen.

Any fear of the fragility of life she'd had was now gone,

and even though she planned to live a long and happy life with Lucca in this lifetime, for as long as she could, Chloe had seen the truth of their afterlives …

There would be no heaven or hell, as their souls would meet again.

EPILOGUE TWO

SOMETIME IN ANOTHER UNIVERSE...

Eira stared up into the blue sky. It looked so vast from up here with nothing in the way to obstruct her view. She could almost reach up and ...

Raising her hand out of the sun-warmed grass, she reached for the clouds, but alas, her arm wasn't long enough to touch them.

With disappointment, she let her hand drop back to earth as her lids became heavy. It might not have been the smartest thing to take a nap on the edge of the cliff, but with her eyes coming to a close, it was rare for Eira to find peace ...

The strangest dream lulled in her mind as she slept, and she would later swear it felt as real as when she was awake. She was dreaming of herself trapped in another body, one of a scarred girl named Chloe, when the nightmares of another life had her jolting awake.

Suddenly rising, she looked out at the edge of the cliff and into the beautiful water that the sun was now setting upon, the blue sky now turned orange. It was a different, breathtakingly beautiful place altogether than when she had fallen asleep.

The fear of the nightmares that weren't hers left her body and were only returned by the sudden deep voice she heard from behind her.

"Hey—"

WHISPERS OF THE DRAGON COMING SOON TO KINDLE VELLA!

REINCARNATE

Don't fear, my darling.
For when I close my eyes for the final time,
I'll meet you in another life.

Please, if you or someone you know ever needs help,
follow this link to get more information and help.

YOU ARE NOT ALONE.

victimsofcrime.org